Mother's Day

Ron Vincent

Mother's Day

Copyright © 2014 by Ron Vincent

A SHORT ON TIME BOOK:

Fast-paced and fun novels for readers on the go!

For more information, visit the website:
www.shortontimebooks.com

I delight in dedicating this book to Elaine. Not a word would have seen the page without your encouragement.

Ten percent of the author's net profits on this book go to the Haven, a shelter for women and children escaping domestic violence. My friends who work there offer hope and encouragement in some of life's darkest moments.

I do not wish to mislead readers with the book's title.

Graphic, strong language occurs more than once inside these pages.

One

I walked down the aisle looking at the Mother's Day cards on display. I pulled out a pop-up card that offered a bouquet of cardboard roses. It read: *I owe you everything.* "That's not quite true," I mumbled to myself. Another card looked more hopeful, a dour black-and-white copy of *Whistler's Mother.* I read aloud, "Gentle, kind and caring are the words I remember when I think of you." My groan caused a young couple to gawk at me.

"Are you OK?" the young man asked.

"Yeah, I'm fine." I ignored their stares and kept looking. On the last rack I found an acceptable card. Happy Mother's Day in block letters with the inside left blank. I bought it.

At the post office I pulled a piece of paper from my pocket and tried to write apt words for the inside of the card. Mom, I know it's been a long time and I forgive you. *Mom, I wish you a happy Mother's Day. I'd like to call you and not have you hang up. Mom, you need to apologize.* I looked at the list of sentences and crossed each one out. I opened the card and wrote: *Sorry about what happened years ago. Your son, Phil.* Forced and dishonest, but better than a blank page. I dropped the card in the mail slot and walked to my car.

Heather didn't greet me when I opened the front door. Her fingers danced across the keyboard as she finished the annual audit of her company's largest client. She reviewed two other documents on her triple-monitor setup. She had five screens in her office across town, but it was more comfortable to sit at home with three screens, a glass of wine, and Slippers, our golden retriever, warming her feet while she scanned endless lines of numbers. Besides, I cooked Southern comfort food better than the Boston restaurant near her office where the chef had no idea what he was doing. She smiled when I walked into the room, tapped *Save*, and gave me a deep, wet kiss.

"Did you send the card?" Heather asked.

"It's done," I confirmed.

"What did you say?"

"Let me get a beer. You want one?" I responded.

"No, but a Riesling would be nice," she answered.

I returned with her wine, my beer, and a tray of cheese. "You finished the report?" I asked.

"Yep, done for another year. So what'd you say in the card?"

"I sent her the damn card, that should make you happy," I barked.

"It isn't about making me happy. It's about you. You need to see her," she insisted firmly.

"I'd rather gargle molten glass. We don't need her in our lives," I growled.

"But maybe she needs us. She's seventy-five," Heather said, leaning back in her chair.

"You left out the best part, she drinks like a fish, and her liver is probably suing her," I shot back.

"You still need to see her." Silence draped the air. I sipped my beer, picked up a book, and dropped into the overstuffed chair.

"I don't want to be a nag—"

"Then don't be!"

"You need to see her. Not for me, not for her, but for you," Heather insisted.

"She ruined our wedding ten years ago and you want me to see her?"

"I just have a feeling, a premonition," she advised.

"Could be the flu," I suggested.

Heather ignored my smartass jab. "You can stop by and see Greg. You two always talk on the phone and make promises to see each other. He is your best friend."

"We can't afford it. Not until I find a job," I disputed.

"We've got more than enough in savings. And we haven't spent a dime of my bonus," Heather reminded me.

"I don't want to spend your bonus," I protested.

"It's our bonus," Heather insisted.

My cell rang and I was grateful for the interruption, until I answered. It was a buddy at a headhunter's office who had promised to find me a job. I listened for a minute then exploded. "Too much experience, too much education! What do these people want? An illiterate who can read specs in three languages for minimum wage? I know you can't make people hire me, but shit!" I threw my phone across the room where it bounced off a chair cushion. Slippers thought it was a game and snatched it out of the air before it slammed into the tile floor.

"You're going to find work again," Heather consoled.

"I have a master's degree and I'm over forty. Too much experience, too much education. They want a fetus who'll work for baby food," I fumed.

"Someone is going to pick you up," Heather tried to calm me.

"And when do you think that will happen?"

"When it happens," Heather answered.

I chugged the beer, walked into the living room and turned on the flat screen TV to a movie channel. I fell asleep and didn't know when Heather covered me with a quilt. I spent the next week emailing hundreds of firms for jobs, searching the internet to find openings that quickly gathered hundreds of applications and closed before I could complete my online application. I walked Slippers in the rain one morning and we both came home soaked. Slippers loved the wetness while I felt like a drenched corpse, useless and futile.

On Friday night, Heather and I argued about me seeing Mom. I didn't budge. When Heather finally went quiet, I assumed the argument was over so I fell asleep on the couch watching a Red Sox game. I didn't know this until later, but Heather went to her computer, opened her browser to a travel page and created an itinerary and reservations for us, but we weren't on the same flight and didn't have the same destination. She printed my boarding pass for Valparaiso Airport, the rental car information, and a copy of my hotel reservation in Crestview, Florida. She made two more calls, packed a suitcase and left a note:

I'm going to spend a week with Glenda in DC at the CPA Conference. You need some time to sort things out, and staying in this house is driving both of us crazy. You need to see your Mom. It's time, and I have a feeling that something good will come from this. I've left you the tickets. They aren't refundable. Please go and call me when you get there. I love you, Heather.

I woke up before dawn to find the tickets and the note on my chest. I looked at my reservation, a red-eye out of Boston that very night. Heather knew that I hate crowded airports and that I liked to sleep on planes. The red-eye suited me, but the date did not fit my ideal, Mother's Day! I had groused over sending a card. I didn't want to send myself. I thought about shredding the ticket and shooting myself in the foot but since I didn't own a gun that seemed problematic . I thought about missing the flight, but I didn't want to waste the money. My cell rang and I recognized the number.

"Hey Greg, How's the law business?" I asked.

"Almost as good as the real estate market. I just read an email from Heather. She said you are on your way to visit me and Lunette. I almost danced a jig. Where do you want to eat supper your first night in Crestview? I was thinking we could go eat flounder in Niceville. Or if you get in early enough, we could do breakfast at the Cracker Barrel. How's that sound to you?" asked Greg.

"It sounds just fine," I agreed.

"What time does your plane get in?" Greg inquired.

We talked for an hour. He'd been the one friend growing up who would come to my house and not make me feel like shit because my mother was drunk. She was always cursing or threatening the neighbors with a rake or looks that could slice the bark off a pine tree. Embarrassment had been central to living with Mrs. Williemaye Oglesby. Greg had been my buddy who never snickered about my tattered clothes, my shoes with holes, or the busted front door. Other kids had been vicious little bastards but never Greg. And in high school, when he became the star quarterback of the football team, he shared his aura. The jeers and cheap shots stopped, at least to my face.

"Are you going to see Williemaye?" asked Greg.

"Yeah, Heather insists," I complained

"Would you like me to come along for the visit?" asked Greg.

"I think that is above and beyond the call of friendship."

"I'm more than willing. Besides, I always liked your mom."

"Greg, no one liked my Mom. You just had a gift for ignoring her," I insisted.

"I did not ignore her. I learned more profanity from Williemaye than I ever picked up as a Marine. I always felt I owed your Mom tuition for what I learned from her."

"Really? You never told me. What would be an example for a tuition-worthy expression?" I inquired.

"You aren't recording this?" asked Greg.

"Greg, I never record conversations with a lawyer," I replied.

"OK, I actually used to go home and write down stuff your mom said. Kept it hidden in a box with a bunch of my favorite comic books. Took the list to college with me. I put it in a file on my computer. Let me see . . . Here's one . . . 'His face would make a dick dripping with syphilis and cow shit look like the blue plate special.' The first time she said that I realized that I was in the presence of greatness. We have statues of people with a lot less talent," Greg revealed.

"Greg, are you drunk?"

"Phil, your Mom was and still is the best cusser I've ever heard. The very best." Greg and I agreed she was good at cussing, and I asked about his kids, his practice, and his parents. He promised a full report when he saw me in Crestview. I had the impression he wanted to talk about something else, so I asked.

"Williemaye's in some trouble," Greg stated.

"She's always in trouble. Nothing new about that," I conceded.

"Phil, this is different. I know the attorney that represents Bank of West Florida, and he mentioned that they're planning to foreclose on your mom's home. I was hoping that Williemaye would have called you. When you said you were coming down, I figured it might be to deal with her problem. Sorry to be the one to tell you but I wanted you to know before you landed in the middle of this mess," Greg supplied.

Two

I landed at the airport before eight in the morning and realized that I had to call Mom, not out of politeness but in self-defense. I needed to know if she was flat on her ass drunk or in a worse-than normal mood before I knocked on her door to wish her an almost sincere happy Mother's Day. Her line rang twenty times before she picked up.

"Who in the hell is this and what in the name of the eternal shit pile do you want?" Mom snarled.

"Mom, it's me. I'm in town and would like to see you," I offered.

"I'm busy right now. But I could use your help a bit later today."

That startled me. Mom never needed my help and she was never busy on Sunday mornings unless she was busy sleeping off the hangover from the night before.

"What can I help you with?" I asked.

"I need you to pick me up from church." I heard the words but I did not hear the sentence.

"I don't understand, Mom."

"Look asshole, pick your flaming mother up from Grace Chapel on 1st Street at 11:45 sharp. You got that?" Mom raged.

"Mom, how long have you been going to this church?"

"That is none of your piss-fucking business, sonny boy. Just don't leave my ass on the curb at 11:45." She hung up.

I called Greg. "Hey guy, I got about three hours to kill before I see Mom. Could you meet me at the Cracker Barrel?"

I pulled into the restaurant parking lot off State Route 85 twenty minutes later. It wasn't full, but the after-church crowd of families in their Sunday best would soon jam every space and every rocking chair on the restaurant-length front porch. This early in the morning, it was full of heathens and those who had to go to work soon. I sat in a rocker and waited for Greg, who was not a churchgoer anymore. He'd bailed after his brother's suicide when a pastor had explained to him in no uncertain terms that Hell greeted all suicides.

A tour bus stopped at the front steps to the porch and disgorged a small horde that, by coming in May, was beating the savage combination of Florida humidity and summer heat. The weather was still tolerable with nights in the sixties and days in the eighties.

I remembered loving May as a kid because it meant I could sleep without soaking my pillow wet with sweat by morning. I dreaded the hottest summer nights when the oppressive heat and one last swallow of Southern Comfort would push Mom into a lost corner of her soul in a vocal nightmare where she screamed at my long-gone father until she was hoarse and her voice faded to a rasping whisper. I was four years old the first time she did that and was convinced that someone must be in her room hurting her. I hid under my bed and waited for the shouting to stop. Then I crawled to her room to see if she was hurt. She was asleep on her belly on the floor with an empty bottle in her hand. All the sheets and covers from her bed were thrown against the wall. Sometime in elementary school around the fourth or fifth grade, I quit checking on her.

I was inside at the table check-in when Greg opened the front door for Lunette and their two kids. The hostess took us to a booth and offered to take our order.

"We'd like two chicken fried steaks with extra gravy and collard greens, and the kids would like the pigs in the blankets. What about you, Phil?"

"Chicken fried steak with collards sounds perfect to me," I agreed.

"We West Florida rednecks do need to stick together," Greg responded.

The server left the kids with crayons and place mats to color while we stirred our coffee. Phil got me up to speed on the state basketball championship we'd won and the baseball championship we'd lost. The food was on the table before Greg finished his history lesson, but when he did finish, Lunette asked the inevitable question Southerners ask all their married friends.

"It's none of my business, but are you and Heather going to have a family?" she inquired.

"Phil, excuse Lunette, she has no sense of boundaries in matters of fertility," said Greg.

"No, no excuses needed. I lost my job six months ago and it just doesn't make sense right now," I explained.

"Phil, it never makes sense but kids add things to a marriage that you can't measure," Lunette said with what appeared to be a smile.

To emphasize her point, her son decided that his little sister needed a pancake with syrup in her hair. His sister did not agree and responded by throwing her milk into his face. Lunette began the marathon clean-up effort coupled with threats of dismemberment. She took the wailing daughter to the restroom while Greg sopped up the milk with extra napkins the smiling server provided. A few minutes later both kids were almost clean, a little tearful, and Lunette reminded the pair that Santa Claus remembered crimes like this, especially crimes committed in the presence of company.

"So, I guess you've already talked to Williemaye this morning. How did she sound?" queried Greg.

"Got a shock when I first got a hold of her," I exclaimed.

"Bet you did," Greg agreed.

"Not that kind of shock. She wants me to pick her up from church." Greg and Lunettee stopped eating.

"Williemaye's at church?" gasped Lunette.

"Grace Chapel," I confirmed.

"Hell has frozen over," Greg declared.

"Has she ever gone to church?" asked Lunette.

"Besides my wedding? No," I answered.

"She could be sick," Greg offered.

"People don't go to church when they're sick," Lunette disputed.

"They did for Oral Roberts," Greg smiled.

"I hadn't thought of that."

We quieted. Maybe Mom's situation was serious but it didn't make sense. Mom had been trying to kill herself for years. She hadn't sounded depressed or religious or anything like that this morning. She'd sounded typical, nasty, self-centered, and a complete bitch. Her attending church just didn't square . . . and that was when I figured it out. She wasn't going to church and she wouldn't be at the curb in front of Grace Chapel at 11:45. She was sleeping one off. Probably emptying another bottle to begin another day, that didn't matter to her any more than my visit did.

"I think she lied to me. She's not at church, unless it's Pastor Jim Beam with the Southern Comfort choir," I sneered.

"So what are you going to do?" asked Greg.

"Well, there's about a one-in-a-million, no, one-in-a-*billion* chance that she's in a church pew by now. If I am not there when she walks out, I'll miss a moment that's on par with the first moon walk. So I'm heading to Krispy Kreme to enjoy a coffee and the morning paper while I wait to see if I'm wrong. I'll give her fifteen minutes before I go by the house to see if she's sober enough to know what century it is," I answered.

Three

I left the Cracker Barrel an hour later and stopped in front of Crestview High School before visiting the Krispy Kreme. I sat in the school's empty parking lot for a few minutes and remembered how much I had loved this place, this haven, because Mom never interrupted a class or came on campus. I was usually the first kid at school and often the last to leave.

The Krispy Kreme was busy. It took ten minutes in line to get a cup of coffee and two jelly doughnuts. It was 11:20 when I parked in front of Grace Chapel on the opposite side of the street. The church's parking lots were filled and all the nearby streets were jammed in all directions. I realized why my spot across the street was open: I was parked next to a fire hydrant. A huge banner fluttered from the front of the church: *Million-Dollar Mother's Day. Join us in an offering that will change people's souls.* I muttered, "It's only gonna change people's wallets."

A patrol car pulled next to me and the officer rolled the window down. "Even though it's Sunday, you can't block a hydrant." The officer stared at me for a moment and I stared back.

"Are you Dwayne Spence?" I asked.

"I surely am and I know you, it's been a long time Phil Oglesby. What are you doing in town?"

"I came to pick up Momma from church."

"Williemaye in church? Never thought I would here those words," replied Dwayne.

"I'm surprised too," I shrugged.

"Don't you live up north these days?"

"Boston."

Dwayne shook his head. "Southern boy like you has no business up there with those people. You belong down here."

"My wife has family up there," I explained.

"Tell her to move down here and they'll more than likely follow her. Them winters up there are plenty cold, aren't they?" Dwayne stated and questioned in the same breath. I admitted that they were and Dwayne decided that he needed to get me up to speed on local politics and the sheriff's office. Seems the last sheriff made an art of embezzlement and was now serving time in a federal prison.

"Our new sheriff's an honest man, a mite excitable, but honest. Hell, he's inside that church right now with your momma," chuckled Dwayne.

I asked Dwayne how he remembered me.

"I was in chemistry with you, Ms. Watkins class. You let me copy your homework or I would've flunked out. Never really thanked you for that help."

We sat in the last row, next to the lab tables," I remembered.

"You're right. Always smelled over there. I also remember the story about your wedding. Didn't your momma sucker punch somebody?"

"My wife's mother. Yeah, she punched her."

"And now she's going to Grace Chapel. People do get funny as they get older," muttered Dwayne.

"You might want to hang around—she might slug someone on the way out," I suggested.

His radio barked to life, announcing an accident on the high-way. "I need to roll. Tell you what, stay put until your Momma comes out but do not leave the car alone. Somebody's likely to tow you if you do." He left with sirens shrieking just as Mom came out the front doors alone.

Four

She shuffled, which passed as a trot for her. Our eyes met as she reached the curb. "Get your ass over here so I don't have to cross no street," she fumed.

I swung the car around and she hopped in with her purse and a large canvas shopping bag.

"And a good morning to you," I bellowed.

"Keep your good morning to yourself," she spat back. Without profanity. Maybe a church service had mellowed her. I sat with the engine running as she settled in. She didn't buckle her seatbelt so I reached over to snap it on.

"I ain't wearing no shit-tarred seatbelt. And get us out of here. I got places to go."

"I can get ticketed if you don't buckle up," I insisted.

"And I will cuss that officer so bad his Momma's ass will catch on fire," Mom assured me.

"I'm not moving until you buckle up."

She filled the air with molten words while she fumbled for the belt. The serene effect of church had worn off very quickly. I pulled away from the curb when I heard the click.

"Did you hit someone again?"

"What in the hell makes you think I hit someone?"

"You've done it before," I answered.

"I have never hit no one inside a church even though there was a couple of bastards in there that looked like a board upside their heads would've done them sonsabitches a world of good," she muttered.

Mom ignored me while she searched through her purse and her shopping bag for something. She was quiet for the ten minutes it took me to drive to her house. When I parked in front, she ignored me for a few moments before her head popped up. "Why in ball-busting tarnation did you bring me here?"

"This is home, Mom. You live here, remember?"

"I want to go to Mossy Head," she insisted.

"Mom, that's fifteen miles away. On a Sunday there can't be anything you need to do in a town that has a general store, two gas pumps, and a trailer park," I replied.

"If you don't take me to Mossy Head, I'm going to walk there," Mom threatened.

I didn't like the idea of being in a car with Mom for fifteen miles plus the fifteen miles back to town. That was too much time in a confined space with her. I thought about dropping her off and letting her walk. I hadn't been subjected to her outbursts for a long time, and my armor was a lot thinner from disuse.

"Would you just take my ass to Mossy Head? I'm too old to walk it but I need to go," Mom insisted.

"Why do we have to go to Mossy Head?" I prodded.

"That's my business. Just drive the duck-fuck car and let me worry about why." I gave up and pulled away from her home. Like almost every road away from the coast, pine trees and scrub oaks lined the highway to Mossy Head. Mom buried her head in the shopping bag for most of the twenty-minute drive. I suspected she had a bottle in the bag and was making up for the time spent not drinking in church. I was grateful for the silence but I knew I had to ask about the foreclosure.

"Mom, I had breakfast at the Cracker Barrel with Greg this morning."

"And why would I give a flying fart about that?" Mom complained.

"He said you are facing a foreclosure on the house."

"And what if I am?"

"Mom, I don't want you to be homeless."

"Who in hell said I was going to be homeless?"

"Mom, when they foreclose, you have to leave your home. You can't stay," I explained

"If I wanted your help with this fermented turd of a mortgage, I would've asked for it. Don't worry your little Boston head about me."

"Mom, they will evict you. They will send sheriff's deputies to carry you out the door, and then they will lock it up," I argued.

"I'll shoot their balls off before they can step on the porch," Mom threatened.

I quit trying to make the point. I passed the sign for Mossy Head, population two hundred thirty three. At the only stop sign, I had two choices: the trailer park or the general store.

"I need to use the general store. You just park in front and leave me alone for a while," Mom instructed.

She left me in the car and took her purse and the bulging shopping bag. I rolled down the windows and fell asleep listening to the cicadas' buzz that filled the air. I began to dream. I was ten years old, walking through the woods behind the house, stopping to turn over tree trunks to find striped lizards and horned beetles. The brilliant sun dappled the forest floor with patches of light. In my reverie I walked into the ten-foot web of a garden spider, a garish yellow-and-black spider the size of a silver dollar. The spider, evidently pissed that I shredded its web, sat squarely on my chin and decided to bite my face. The bite in my dream coincided with a very real yellow fly who had decided to enjoy her blood lunch on my chin. The romance of the country ended when I slapped the fly in time to squash it against my face. A glance in the rear view mirror showed that I looked like someone had shot me. I needed to use the Mossy Head General Store bathroom, whether it was public or not. I glanced at my watch. I had dozed for forty-five minutes, and Mom was still inside.

The general store looked like it had been borrowed from Andy Griffith. It had a little of everything: tackle and bait, a snack bar with fried catfish and hush puppies—fried pies with fillings so sweet they'd hurt your teeth—and an assortment of first aid goods, detergents, hunting caps, shotgun shells, and boxes with frozen foods. One corner of the store featured an ATM for the Bank of West Florida. The store contents were under the gaze of a herd of stuffed animal heads including wild boar, deer, bobcats, and black bears. Mom was stooped over the ATM with her head plunged into the shopping bag. The bored clerk stood at one of two cash registers eating a pecan-filled fried pie and drinking a two-liter soda while watching the news broadcast from Pensacola. A large sign over the top of the bathroom door in the back read: *Only for our customers.* I tried the door, but it was locked.

"Can I have the restroom key?"

The clerk eyed me as she gulped down a mouthful of fried pie. "You have to buy something."

I looked over at Mom, wondering why her head still bobbed in the shopping bag. "Mom, would you like a soda?"

"Get me a Dr Pepper and then leave me the flaming hell alone," she replied.

I paid for the soda and handed it to Mom, who had finally come up for air. She took the soda and set a stack of bills on the small counter next to the ATM. I glanced at the stack, a wad almost three inches high capped with a hundred-dollar bill. She had five such stacks in a line on the little counter. Discarded checks littered the floor, so I picked one up. It was made out to Grace Chapel for one thousand dollars. I picked up another one. Made out to Grace Chapel for fifty dollars. Mom tossed another to my feet and began to feed a stack of bills into the ATM.

"Mom, what in the hell are you doing with all this money and these checks from Grace Chapel?"

"I ain't doing nothing with the checks. Only the cash. Them checks is worthless to me," Mom answered without a glimmer of concern.

"Mom, they didn't give you this money."

"You little nosey bastard, as if it was any of your business. I took it before I left," Mom answered with heat.

"Mom, they didn't just give you all this. Did you steal it when no one was looking?"

"Oh, they was looking when I took it. They was looking at this," Williemaye grinned as she showed me an old .38 long-barrel revolver. "Now, go bother that cashier or go piss in a corner somewhere."

I went to the cashier, who was watching the news on a small flat-screen TV just above her register. Before I could say a word to her, a bulletin banner interrupted the weather man on the screen. The next scene showed a news truck parked in an ocean of police cars in front of Grace Chapel while a reporter talked on camera. The cashier turned up the volume.

The reporter held her mic to Deputy Dwayne. "A woman robbed Grace Chapel this morning after the Mother's Day offering. We have been unable to speak to anyone who saw the robbery. The sheriff is interviewing those people as we speak. I do have a deputy sheriff who is willing to provide us with the current update."

"We got a suspect in mind but we need to be sure before we release any descriptions," Dwayne offered.

"Did a single person commit this crime?" asked the reporter.

"We're not going to speculate at this time," answered Dwayne.

"We've heard that it was an elderly woman who used a gun. Can you comment on that?"

"I'm gonna let Sheriff Robbie handle the more detailed announcement."

Another deputy sauntered over and whispered into Dwayne's ear, and Dwayne quickly left. The newswoman found a man in a nearby crowd who wanted to speak.

"I don't know what America has come to when some old woman robs a church on Mother's Day. I just don't know what to say," the man complained.

"Did you see the woman who did this?"

"See her? She set next to me!" the man supplied.

Mom looked over at me and yelled, "I could use some help, you little bastard."

I leaned over to the cashier. "I think my Mom robbed that church," I whispered. The cashier looked at Mom with wonder.

"Who in the hell do you think you're staring at? I ain't Miss Big Titties America, so look somewhere else if you want to stare at someone, you dumb bitch!" Mom yelled. The cashier picked up her cell and scampered outside. I trotted over to Mom, who fed bills into the machine and asked me to hand her another stack. The screen revealed her balance: eighty-four thousand, nine hundred eighty dollars.

"Mom, the police know about the robbery. People know you stole that money," I warned.

"Don't matter. I don't care what people know as long as they keep their snot-drooling noses out of my business," Mom replied.

"Mom, you're going to get arrested for this," I told her.

"Well, happy buzzard-pissing Mother's Day to you too. Helluva way to talk to me on the one damn day a year reserved for all the sack-of-shit mothers in this little corner of paradise."

"Mom, stop putting the money into the ATM. It isn't yours!"

"I ain't stoppin' nothin'. I stole this money fair and square, and if you are so delicate that it twists your jockey strap sideways to see your momma with some cash, you just go outside and piss on yourself," Mom answered.

I gave up the conversation and walked over to the flat screen TV, which showed the reporter talking to Sheriff Robbie.

"We believe we have a positive identification. This morning, a woman in her seventies used a revolver to rob Grace Chapel at approximately 11:42 a. m. We are not sure at this time if she had accomplices inside the church, but one of our deputies has identified the getaway car as a rental. He also believes that he knows the driver and the woman . . ."

Williemaye Oglesby's picture flashed on the screen: *Crestview woman robs local church. Ushers say an undetermined amount of cash stolen.* Gut-punched, numb, and betrayed I sat on the stool at the cashier's station and stared at Mom. She kept feeding cash into the ATM, tossing checks to the floor, and drinking her soda. Outside, the cashier paced back and forth while she talked on the phone, likely to the police. I wanted to wring Mom's neck and turn back the clock to the moment when I was boarding the plane in the Boston terminal. I wished I had walked out of that terminal. I wished I had skipped Mother's Day in Crestview. My cell rang, startling me out of my wishful thinking. Heather.

"Hello Phil, I just wanted to see how you and Mom were doing?" I didn't speak. "Can you hear me, Phil?"

"I can hear you. I just don't know what to say. It can't be that bad. You just need to give her a chance."

"Right now I'd like to give her the electric chair."

"Phil, you really need to try." Sirens blared in the distance. The symphony of wails suggested that the Mossy Head General Store oyster-shell-of-a parking lot was not large enough to accommodate the thirty vehicles converging on it.

"What are those sirens about?" asked Heather.

"Mom, they're about Mom."

"Oh no! Has she had a heart attack?" asked Heather.

"I don't think I could get that lucky."

"That is a horrible thing to say," Heather rebuked.

"No, it's not. You need to know something . . . I think Mom robbed a church this morning and I picked her up after the robbery. I am in deep shit and I don't have a shovel."

"Phil, I don't think this is funny. You're not telling me the truth." The patrol cars with their sirens shrieking jammed the parking lot. Some officers couldn't open their doors because they had slid in so tightly next to other cars. I ended the call.

Five

The cashier ran to the first patrol car that stopped. She pointed at me in the doorway and shouted, "They're inside!" Cars were so tightly parked that officers could only bang their doors against their neighbors' cars in a futile effort to jump out of their own units. Deputy Dwayne parked on the other side of the street and helped the officers back up their cars so that the adrenaline-charged cavalry could swing out of their seats to point their 9mm guns, pump shotguns, and Uzis at me. More than a dozen officers aimed their weapons at me and—like the village idiot—I stared back at the wannabe firing squad. Mom might have saved my life when she yelled for me.

"Get your ass crack over here and help me." I held up my hands and backed away from the open door. No one fired but more officers joined the front ranks with shotguns, AR-15s, and at least one grenade launcher.

"Mom, do you know what you've done?" Mom handed me the shopping bag. After all the bills she'd fed the ATM, her shopping bag still overflowed with cash.

"I needed a loan," she said.

"Mom! Churches don't make loans!"

"One did this morning."

"Mom, you robbed a church. That's not a loan!" I yelled.

"They wanted to give their money to God, and I just figured He could afford me taking some before it got into His pockets," Mom disputed.

My cell rang and I answered it, expecting Heather. It wasn't.

"Phil? It seems real likely that Williemaye done robbed Grace Tabernacle this morning," said Deputy Dwayne.

"Well Dwayne, I have the same impression." Mom reached inside the shopping bag, grabbed a handful of bills, and began sorting them into neat piles on the counter.

"Mom, damnit. Stop it." She ignored me and grabbed more bills.

"Phil, what's going on in there?" asked Dwayne.

"Mom's putting the offering into the ATM," I answered.

"Did she pray first?" asked Dwayne with a chuckle.

"No, Mom's not the praying type." She fed another stack of bills into the machine.

"You suppose you two could come out without a lot of ruckus?" asked Dwayne.

"Mom, the deputy would like you to come outside with me."

"Put that phone on speaker for a minute," Mom said. I put the cell on speaker and Mom leaned in. "All you sonsabitches go home and fondle your mommas cause I ain't comin' out of here until I'm ready to come out. You hear?" Mom turned back to the counter and fed more bills to the ATM.

"Dwayne, I don't think she's comin' out for a while."

"Why don't you come out then?"

Mom looked at me and spit on the floor, then offered another pearl of wisdom. "Go ahead, join them morons outside. They ain't got enough brains out there to bell a buzzard and maybe if you go out there and help them, they can unzip their pants before they go and wet on themselves."

"Mom, this is the dumbest shit you have ever pulled. You need to end it now before someone gets hurt."

Mom stooped and pulled out a snubnosed .38 from her purse, then pointed it at me.

"If you can't shut your mouth long enough for me to count money, I'm gonna have to shoot you. So just go ahead and leave." She grabbed one more handful of bills from her stash, then handed me the shopping bag. It wasn't empty.

"What do you expect me to do with this?" I asked.

"I got enough with what I got left here to take care of my business. Go give it to the morons outside and knowin' how stupid they are you can help them count it. It'll give them something to do before Barney Fife shows up and tells them all how to wipe their asses."

I walked to the open front door with the shopping bag. The SWAT truck was blocking the road, and black-fatigued officers covered me on all sides as I stepped into the parking lot. Deputy Dwayne walked toward me and softly spoke. "Everyone's a little touchy, so just raise your hands slowly." I followed his advice while Sheriff Robbie bellowed over his bullhorn, "I want you to empty that sack right now. I ain't gonna go out with no suicide bomber."

I emptied the sack, and the stiff afternoon breeze blew money in every direction. Hundred-dollar bills floated above the store's roof. Fifties fled across the road and roosted in the branches of tall pine trees. Signed checks scattered in the breeze. Months later, a hunter found a squirrel's nest lined with four thousand dollars in what had once been on an offering plate. But the immediate effect was chaos. Sheriff Robbie screamed, "Get the dagburned money!" before a wad of bills blew into his bullhorn. A swath of bills blew into the back of a satellite news truck as the camera operator and reporter exited the rear doors. The camera operator panned the scene, filming deputies and SWAT in hot pursuit of the cash.

I stood my ground until two deputies tackled me, slapped on a pair of handcuffs, and dragged me into a squad car. The news reporter waited for the officers to join the others snatching cash across the road, then she tapped the camera operator on the shoulder and he quickly pointed his lens at my face inside the car. She tapped on the window and spoke, "Could you explain what we just saw?" I tried to answer through the glass but she couldn't hear my response so I gave up and shrugged. She looked around like a child stealing candy and opened the front doors to the squad car. The camera operator settled into the driver's seat, moved the riot gun out of the way and filmed the interview between me and the reporter.

"Let's try again. Where did all this money come from?" she asked.

"It was in the shopping bag until the sheriff ordered me to turn it upside down," I answered.

"How did it get into the shopping bag?"

"You'd have to ask my mother that question."

"Where is she?" the reporter asked.

"Inside the store with a .38 revolver and a Dr Pepper," I said as a fifty dollar bill blew into my face. The reporter made sure that her camera guy filmed the shot before she removed the bill from where it had settled just above my shirt collar.

"The authorities are alleging that your mother may have robbed a church this morning. Can you comment on that?" she asked.

"I'm sitting in the back of a police car with handcuffs and you want me to talk about something my mother might have done? What I want to know is why in Heaven's shit tent I'm sitting here with handcuffs. I'd like to know the answer to that question."

"Could you tell me how old your mother is?"

"Williemaye is seventy-five."

"Has she ever done anything like this before?"

"I haven't seen her in ten years. I don't know what she's been doing."

"Why haven't you seen your mother for so long?"

"Because I haven't," I said.

"This story isn't about me. It's about you and her. I wish you would cooperate." The reporter tapped her camera guy on the shoulder and gestured at her throat to cut the recording. He lowered the camera. "You need all the good karma you can get. I can make you look a victim to our viewers. That can't hurt you in your situation. What do you say?"

I didn't know what to do. The reporter looked less sincere than a used car salesman who moonlighted as a pimp and part-time televangelist. Sheriff Robbie was collecting cash with a burlap sack, and no one in particular was watching the Mossy Head General Store. No one but me saw Mom slip out of the front door and meander among the parked police units until she found one that had something she wanted. She tossed a rifle from the front seat to the ground, then a box of ammo, and finally a riot gun. I could not figure out what in the hell she was

29

doing until she disappeared below the window line then reappeared with a bull horn and calmly walked back into the store. Our eyes locked as she looked my way. She was smiling.

Six

Sheriff Robbie saw red when he noticed the reporter in the back seat with me. He opened the car door with his gun drawn and aimed at me.

"What in tarnation are you doing talking to the press?"

"I didn't invite them to this party. They invited themselves," I answered.

"I'm a reporter and we just want to keep the public informed," she stated.

"And I'm the county sheriff and you are talking to my prisoner without my permission," Robbie replied indignantly.

Dwayne walked up to the car. Sheriff Robbie glanced at his deputy and made a command decision.

"I want you to sit Phil's ass in your patrol car and stay with him," said the sheriff, not noticing that the reporter had motioned for her camera operator to go live again.

Sheriff Robbie roared, "I want you to shoot these people if they so much as get within pissing distance of your unit. I don't want no hand signs, cardboard signs, or deaf interpreters so much as looking at Phil in your back seat. Are we all perfectly clear on this situation?"

Dwayne wordlessly escorted me to his car while the reporter and her crew taped my brief march to a more secure car. I sat in the back seat and wondered whether or not to tell Dwayne that Mom had rummaged through one of the units, tossing weapons to the ground until she found a bullhorn. I decided to keep quiet.

With all the bourbon in the store and a bullhorn, she might serenade us with Top 40 hits from the fifties or simply use the device to project her profanity further than its usual distance. I wasn't exactly sure what she would do. What decided it for me was the CNN truck. They pulled up across the road right next to the SWAT van. With this much network coverage, I figured the level of testosterone-poisoning was rising and the officers outside the store were going to start treating this like the Alamo, without realizing that Jim Bowie in drag waited inside with only a .38 and a case of Old Granddad.

"Dwayne, you might need to know that Mom walked out of the store a few minutes ago."

"Why in the hell didn't you say something?"

"I'm working on that if you'll let me finish. She walked over to that car by those pine trees and fished out a bullhorn and took it back inside," I answered.

"That beats it all. We're out chasing the damn money because Sheriff Robbie is an idiot for having you dump that bag, and we miss a chance to grab her without having to storm the store. Do you know if she knows how to shoot that pistol she's got?" asked Dwayne.

"I have no idea if she could hit the broad side of a barn or a flea in the ass at twenty yards," I responded.

Before Dwayne and I could further discuss Mom's ability to shoot, Sheriff Robbie announced a decision from across the road over his open-vest microphone. He said, "It would save the county a lot of trouble if we just sent SWAT in to kill her and be done with this mess. Somebody like this might have a bomb or some kinda weapon of mass destruction or IED."

Dwayne cut into the conversation over his mic, "Shit, Robbie, all the old biddy has is a .38."

"And how in the hell do you know that?" spat back the sheriff.

"Damnit to hell Robbie, that's all the old lady's got," Dwayne insisted.

"Shit," the Sheriff said.

My cell rang. Dwayne reached into the back seat and pulled it out of my jacket. He saw Heather's name and answered for me.

"Hey Heather, this is Dwayne Spence. That's right, I was at your wedding. Phil sort of dropped his phone and I picked it up for him. Just give him a minute." Dwayne slid out of the front seat and opened my door, unlocked the handcuffs, handed me the phone, and stood outside the car.

"What are you doing?"

"I'm in the back of Dwayne's squad car under arrest."

"Phil, I'm tired of these jokes. I know you didn't want to go down there, but this stunt where you tell me you are in a police car after hanging up on me—I know you're under pressure from losing your job but that's no reason to treat me like this."

"Heather, turn on Headline News," I instructed.

"I don't watch TV," Heather argued.

"Turn on the news and you'll see that CNN is covering the Mossy Head General Store. You might even be able to see the car I'm sitting in," I informed her.

Seven

Heather told me later that she turned on CNN to see Sheriff Robbie knock the cell phone out of my hands and to catch the shouting match that followed between him and Deputy Dwayne.

"You ain't got no business lettin' him on the phone!" screamed the sheriff.

"We need Phil's help to end this thing inside the store," Dwayne argued.

"His help? You moron, he's why we got this problem inside the store!"

I decided to help Dwayne. "Sheriff, it was just my wife in Chicago. That was all that was."

"Phil Oglesby, my wife taught you in second grade. And look at this mess," said Robbie.

"This isn't my fault," I countered.

"I don't see nobody else to blame. Helpin' your own mother rob a church on Mother's Day!" screamed Robbie.

"All I did was pick her up. "

"You can put that crap in a can of Prince Albert and toss it into the Chatahoochee River," said Robbie.

Mom interrupted our conversation with her bullhorn.

"Hey all you sonsabitches, I'd like a pepperoni pizza."

Sheriff Robbie replied on his bullhorn. "Williemaye Oglesby, you did a really bad thing today. You ought to be ashamed of yourself. I'm asking you real nice to please come outside so I don't have to ask my boys to shoot your ass off!"

"I ain't coming out or even thinking about coming out until I get a pizza. And as for shooting my ass off, your deputies have a hard time jerking off with their wives. I don't think they could hit a donkey in the ass with a baseball bat if it was as dead as Julius fuckin' Caesar," Williemaye cursed.

"There ain't pizzas around here, Williemaye," yelled Robbie over his bullhorn.

"You sure as shit got enough deputies out there that you can afford to send one shit-faced clown to Jimmy's Pizza in Crestview," answered Mom.

"I'm not doing that. Got no reason to. And I do not appreciate you describing my deputies as shit-faced clowns," Robbie complained.

"I'm just describing what they are and I don't pissant care whether you like it or not," said Mom.

I sat in the car and listened. Mom wasn't going to come out. Not anytime soon at least. She loved to piss people off and she had a gift for it. This was her masterpiece.

A SWAT officer tapped Sheriff Robbie on the shoulder and the two walked to what I supposed was the command post at the armored van. Dwayne picked up my cell from beside the squad car. Sheriff Robbie knocked the battery out of it. Dwayne put the battery back and tried to turn the phone on. A diagonal crack ran across the screen. The phone didn't work.

"I had no idea she'd robbed the church when I picked her up," I explained.

"I believe you. This is just a technicality we have to work out. You got a problem with the cashier inside the store. She's going to be testifyin' about this and all she has to say is that you brought Williemaye here to put money in the ATM. It may not matter too much to a jury or a judge that you don't see it that way. Didn't you think it was a might peculiar for her to be puttin' that much money into an ATM on a Sunday?" Dwayne asked.

"Peculiar is her middle name. "

"I'll give you that," Deputy Dwayne agreed. "It would help a lot if she would just come out. If she doesn't, they will go in and get her."

"I don't care if they send in the 82nd Airborne Division," I responded.

"Given what I've seen of Williemaye so far, I'm not sure they would be very successful," said Dwayne.

My arms hurt like hell by now. The handcuffs were digging into my wrists, and the arthritis from my basketball games in college made my knees feel like charcoal was burning on top of them. Dwayne looked around and slipped into the back seat with me. "Would you be willing to take a stab at talking her out?" Dwayne asked.

"Why would I want to do that?"

"She's your mother."

"That's not my fault."

"We really need your help whether the sheriff is smart enough to know it or not. Somebody could get hurt bad," Dwayne answered.

"She's never given a butterfly's fart about me—"

"We're going to do this together and you're in regardless," said Dwayne, pointing at a SWAT team flanking the store and headed around back.

Eight

The sheriff was lost in conversation with a half-dozen officers and men in suits, so he didn't see Dwayne unlock my cuffs as I stood outside the car. He didn't see us go around the corner of the store to the back. We found the SWAT team huddled together checking their MP5 submachine guns.

"Boys, what in the hell do you think you're doing?" asked Dwayne.

"We're about to take this bitch down," the lieutenant commented.

"You fellers kill an old lady on Mother's Day, even if she is a crazy old coot, and you'll never live it down," Dwayne pointed out.

"Old lady? We heard she was with al-Qaeda and has a bomb!" responded the lieutenant.

"My mom has a .38 pistol with bullets older than all of you," I informed him

"I've got orders to go in there and resolve this." Sweat dripped from the lieutenant's chin strap.

Deputy Dwayne leaned over to him and whispered for several minutes. The lieutenant's face was blank the whole time until he stepped away and waved his crew back. We went inside the store, and Dwayne left his pistol strapped in his holster.

Dwayne let me walk in front of him, which turned out to be a mistake. Walking from the brightly lit outdoors into the dim storage area near the back of the store, I was momentarily blinded. I didn't see the cat sleeping in the middle of the aisle but I heard it when I stepped on its tail. Its scream startled Dwayne, who jerked to one side and toppled a pyramid of cans.

"What dumb sonofabitch is playing with hisself back there?" bellowed Williemaye.

"Mom, Deputy Dwayne and I are here to talk."

"You two haven't got enough brains between you to empty a shit sack into a cesspool."

"Mom, we're coming down this aisle and don't want to get shot," I shouted.

Mom was silent. I motioned to Dwayne to stay still. I knew she was deciding whether or not to shoot.

"Mom, don't shoot," I shouted again.

"Alright, you stupid bastards. I won't shoot," she sighed.

"Your momma always refer to you as a bastard?" Dwayne whispered.

"That's one of the nicer things she's called me."

Mom was sitting in the cashier's high chair at the register with the .38 in one hand and a bottle of bourbon in the other. She took a swig and set the bottle down next to a six-pack of Dr Pepper. She opened a can and filled the half-empty bourbon bottle. She sampled her concoction and smiled. "Always feel better when I mix Dr Pepper with my bourbon. Now, what do you got to say to me with half the damn deputies in Okaloosa County outside this store hankering to shoot me in the ass?"

"Mrs. Oglesby, no one wants to shoot you," Dwayne disputed.

"Then they must just be planning a picnic and an early Fourth of damn July. I hope they invited Willie Nelson." She took another drink.

"Mrs. Olglesby, you've got a gun and they're afraid you'll use it," Dwayne explained.

"I just might do that." Mom took another swig from her bottle.

"Williemaye, if you don't cooperate Phil has a very good chance of being charged as an accomplice in the armed robbery of a church. You know what kind of sentence that brings in these parts?" asked Dwayne.

"Phil didn't do shit. He just picked me up. He wouldn't even help me with the ATM, little bastard," Mom complained.

"Look, Williemaye, the sooner you walk out of here peacefully and tell people the whole truth, the better it will be for everyone," Dwayne urged.

"Truth? People don't know the truth when it bites them in the ass and holds on. It's like pissing into a hurricane. You don't get the truth, you just get piss wet." Mom took another gulp.

I looked out the front window. A bald fat guy with NEGOTIATOR in bold yellow letters on his black flak jacket was talking to the sheriff and a SWAT officer. The negotiator stepped back from the group and tapped on his cell phone. The phone at the register rang an instant later. Dwayne answered.

"This is Deputy Dwayne here, what can I do for you?" Dwayne frowned as he listened, then looked out the window at the negotiator and waved at him.

"I think I can handle this just fine if you give me a few minutes, Mr. Negotiator." The negotiator pointed his finger at

Dwayne and shook his head so hard I thought he might bust a vein.

"You're takin' over on whose authority?" Dwayne put the store phone on speaker.

"I'm taking over because the lieutenant governor is in on this one. You understand me, boy?" snarled the negotiator.

Mom listened to every word. Her smile nearly broke her face as she cut in. "You mean some shit-eatin' political whore in Tallahassee is tryin' to get his nose up my ass?"

The negotiator retorted, "I have orders—"

"Tell that piss-lipped, puss-gutted, slick-haired sonofabitch that Mrs. Williemaye Oglesby ain't got no use for him and the other putrid turds in Tallahassee, and that lieutenant governors mean less to me than composted cow shit. And you can tell him what I just said word for word you little snot-faced, butt-lipped lizard. Now crawl back to your momma and the shit pile she lives in and leave me the hell alone." Mom reached down with her free hand, turned the speaker off, and took the phone off the hook.

Out in the parking lot, the negotiator stood in the sun looking like someone had kicked him in the crotch and beat him with a pipe wrench. He leaned against a car until a deputy opened the car door and eased him into the passenger seat. Robbie tried to start a conversation, but the negotiator seemed lost and paid no attention at all to the sheriff. Robbie gave up and called Dwayne.

Dwayne said, "Look Robbie, I understand this thing's gotten political but if you can keep these fellows off my back for about thirty minutes, I think we can do this without anyone getting hurt or making more of a mess than we already have."

I couldn't hear what Robbie said back, but Dwayne's reply filled in the gap. "If I don't pull it off, you just go ahead and let that negotiator wear himself out." Dwayne turned his cell off. Mom drank more of her Bourbon Dr Pepper and tore open a bag of salted peanuts with her teeth. She poured the peanuts into the bourbon bottle, then added soda and warm beer to the mix. She chugged about two inches of the mixture and started chewing the peanuts left in her mouth.

"Williemaye, why did you rob that church?" asked Dwayne.

"I needed some money," Mom replied.

"What for?"

"You know damn well what for! To keep those vomit-eating buzzards at the bank from auctioning my house away from me."

"I don't see this crime stopping them," Dwayne answered.

"Already done it," Mom explained.

I had to ask a question. "Mom, how did you do that?"

"Right here at that friggin' ATM."

"Mom, you cannot deposit that much cash at one time and then pay off a mortgage. It doesn't work like that," I shook my head in disbelief.

"I did today," Mom stated with satisfaction.

"Mom, I don't think so—"

"Mrs. Oglesby, if you've accomplished what you set out to do, why don't we walk outside and take a break from all this excitement. I'd like to have dinner with my wife and her mother," Dwayne suggested.

"I don't give a gnat's piss about you, your wife, or your momma," Mom snarled.

41

"My momma is dead so if you don't mind, I'd like you to leave her out of this," Dwayne insisted

"Nobody tells me what to say! Nobody. And besides, I can solve all this for everyone right now without taking a step outside." Mom put the .38 revolver to her temple and stared me squarely in the eyes. "Wouldn't you like this as my Mother's Day present to you? Me shootin' myself ought to please you to no end. You wouldn't have to think about me no more."

Nine

Mom held the gun to her head, her hand slightly trembling. Her mother had died of Parkinson's disease, and it had begun with the same shaking in her right hand. My grandmother had been a Southern Baptist deacon's daughter who had run away from home pregnant with my mother. She made a living in the thirties and forties as a stripper and later as a madam in a whorehouse across the state line in Alabama. She'd lived with us at the end and died in her sleep when I was five.

Mom held the gun to her head until she needed another drink. She swapped hands and emptied the bourbon bottle. "I feel better. I don't think I want to shoot myself just yet. But I would dearly like to shoot someone today. Missed my best chance with one of those stuffy ushers at that church."

A hiss and a half growl crept up behind me. I turned to see an opossum charging toward us with foam on its grinning muzzle. Dwayne reached for his 9mm but before he could clear leather, Mom fired one shot. The opossum fell dead with a bullet through one eye. Blood leaked onto the worn linoleum floor. Outside, officers scrambled at the sound of the shot and Sheriff Robbie roared orders with his bullhorn. "Call the EMTs, somebody inside's been shot! I want the SWAT team to storm the building now! Shoot to kill!" A spotter pointed at Mom, whose laser-dotted forehead revealed she was framed in someone's crosshairs. She laid the revolver on the counter and gave the spotter and his shooter the finger.

Dwayne shouted into his mic, "She shot an opossum! Damn it to hell! She shot an opossum! Everyone stand down. You dumb sonsabitches." He threw an evil look at Williemaye and said, "Now there you go, you've got me talking like you."

The reporter and her camera crew took advantage of the confusion and charged the front door. The camera operator got a close-up of the dead opossum, Dwayne shouting into his mic, and me wishing I had joined the French Foreign Legion so I could die peacefully in some godforsaken hell hole where no one knew me or my mother.

Mom turned to the camera and grinned. "Y'all come to see the desperado who declared war on the rabid possum?"

Dwayne drew his pistol and waved it in the general direction of the camera crew. "I'm going to arrest all of you and drive you to Crestview tied to the hood of my car if you don't get out of here right now!" The reporter stared at Dwayne without budging. Her camera operator panned the scene and tried for a close-up of Mom, who noticed she was out of bourbon and grabbed a bottle from a display while trying to steady herself with her other hand. Dwayne reacted in a blink. He scooped the gun off the counter and slipped it into his pocket. Before Mom fully understood what was happening, he had her bound in a pair of handcuffs. The reporter and her crew caught all of it.

I expected Mom to curse a blue streak, but instead she favored shrieking, kicking, stomping, and more shrieking. I could only make out several fragments—"whore bastards" said with two syllables in the first word and the second, and the words exploded with such force it sucked the air out of the room. On her way out, Mom saw Sheriff Robbie and screamed something about shitting on his face in hell but I couldn't be sure because her screaming distorted every word into a verbal, abstract brushstroke that made clarity impossible. I stepped out behind her with Dwayne hanging on to her for all he was worth. Outside, half a dozen deputies lunged to help him. Mom managed to kick one in the crotch before the swarm of hands on her rendered further harm impossible. I stood on the front porch of the store as the swarm carried her to a police van where she was strapped in and muzzled in a melee of uncoordinated confusion.

The camera crew caught all of it.

When it was over, the reporter directed her attention to me. She shoved her microphone in my face and asked one question before a scrum of deputies swept me away. "Is your mother crazy?" She followed me to Dwayne's unit and tried to continue the interview as I sat in handcuffs in the back seat with the window rolled up. "Is Williemaye Oglesby crazy?" she asked again. I didn't know what to say. Crazy was normal to me. Until I'd left Crestview for college, crazy was where I'd lived, where I'd slept, and where I'd woken up every morning.

The van with Mom left the parking lot with lights flashing and sirens wailing. Dwayne sat with me for the thirty minutes it took to uncoil the traffic mess surrounding the general store. We didn't say much to each other. About halfway through the wait he opened the back door, took off the handcuffs, and told me to sit in the front passenger seat.

"Dwayne, this could get you in some trouble."

"Don't care. I campaigned for Robbie, and the difference between him winning and losing the election was about equal to all my relatives who vote in the county. He might not like everything

I do, but he likes winning elections more than just about any man I've ever met. So I don't see a lot of trouble in my future with Sheriff Robbie." We sat until almost everyone else had left, then Dwayne pulled out into the late afternoon shadows.

Six satellite TV vans lined the curb in front of the courthouse and jail annex in downtown Crestview. Locals gathered to watch. Dwayne tried to keep me out of the limelight by parking in the side lot, but someone must have figured out that I had not been booked because the moment my head popped out of the squad car, camera floodlights nearly blinded me. I stumbled over to Dwayne and spoke into his ear.

"You have got to handcuff me. I don't care how much Robbie owes you. You've been my friend in this mess and I don't want you hurt." We faced our backs to the cameras so nobody could record Dwayne cuffing my hands in front of me. The walk through the lot to the side door was slower than a snail's crawl with reporters, cameras, and gawkers unwilling to clear a path for us. Dwayne finally lowered his head and bulled his way through the crowd. He knocked one camera operator off his feet to reach the door.

Dwayne took me to Processing and removed the cuffs again. The man at the desk looked up at me and shook his head. "Phil Oglesby, you're the last man I ever expected to see the inside of a jail. You don't remember me, do you? I'm Tommy Hartsell, we were in Civics class as seniors."

"I sat in back and didn't see much of that class from there," I replied.

Mom interrupted from a room next door. Whoever was in charge of intake processing for women was getting a profanity lesson that boomed through the thin partition. "I don't give a tomcat's scrotum that you are a Christian woman and that my language offends your holy ass. This is a jail, you dumb bitch, not a Sunday school. If you don't like hearing me say damn, shit, puss-faced, and puke-prick all in the same sentence, then find some deaf sonofabitch who ain't quite so delicate. Holy Moses, to think your Daddy was so stupid as to crawl into a bed and screw some gap-toothed, ditch-bank whore to make you!"

The woman exploded in tears, and a door slammed shut. Dwayne looked at the rattling whiteboard and shook his head. "They thought Marabelle Spencer could do intake with Williemaye? Somebody didn't think."

"Who's Marabelle?" I asked.

"She's new and just over from the Juvenile Center. Profanity upsets her," Dwayne explained.

"And she's in this line of work?"

"Like I said, she's new. I better go handle this before somebody decides to mace Williemaye."

He left me with Tommy, who sped through the forms on the computer screen while he asked all the mandatory questions.

When Tommy asked me to empty my pockets, I put the cell phone on the desk but he pushed it back to me. "Phil, make your phone call and make it count."

"Why is this one so important?"

"Because you only get one call a week and once I lock you up, it's from a pay phone that charges three dollars a minute," Tommy informed.

"Three dollars a minute? That's robbery!" I complained.

"I am inclined to agree. Make your call." I called Heather.

"Hello hon', I'm in jail," I began.

"This is insane. They can't keep you," Heather contended.

"I think they're real serious about keeping me."

"What can I do?" asked Heather.

"Call Greg and have him come by. Maybe he can post bail or get these charges dropped."

"What are the charges?" asked Heather.

I asked Tommy to answer that question and held the cell toward him. He read from my intake doc, "Armed robbery, felony aiding and abetting, felony grand theft, felony conspiracy to commit armed robbery, crossing interstate lines to commit a felony, and I'm expecting the DA to add some more in the morning. Unless things get cleared up, I don't expect you to be looking at bail. Not for a while at least. Did you hear all that, Mrs. Oglesby?"

Heather assured me that she'd heard all of it. "I'm going to leave the conference in the morning. I can make connections in Atlanta and be there tomorrow afternoon. I'm sorry. I ruined Mother's Day for you. "

"Actually, Mom ruined it," I countered.

"If I had left you alone, you'd be at home," she cried. I didn't want to agree with her but it was true. I was going to spend my first night back in my hometown in jail; my only comfort was that I would not have to spend it in a cell with Mom.

"I'll call Greg as soon as you hang up," Heather promised. I grunted a "love you" in response, and she whispered one back in return. I handed my cell to Tommy.

Tommy led me through a door to a room with a steel bench attached to a cement wall. A guard with an electronic wand waved it from my toes to my head and motioned for me to undress as he tossed me a bag with a barcode tag for everything I was wearing. Once naked, I learned what the phrase strip search meant as another guard with rubber gloves checked every orifice for contraband. He peered into each ear as if I had hidden an IED in my ear canals. The rest of me took a lot longer to inspect. Screaming about the absurdity of the search seemed like a good idea until I realized that four guards the size of NFL linemen had entered the cubicle and stood in reserve, ready to greet any resistance with over a half ton of muscle. I almost relaxed. The guard supervised my shower and handed me an orange jumpsuit emblazoned with Crestview County Jail.

The only surprise that first night was that I slept in a cell by myself. I expected cell mates but that didn't happen until the next day. I spent most of the night awake but when I did fall asleep, an old memory made it a restless sleep. I was twelve and waiting at the bus stop a block from my house. The bus was about to stop when Mom came running toward me wearing a housecoat and flip-flops. She got to me before the bus did and she began yelling at me before the driver opened the door.

"Did you take my whiskey money, you little bastard? Did you take my money?" she screamed.

"No, Mom. I didn't take your money," I answered meekly.

The bus door opened and I plunged inside so fast that I stumbled and my legs stuck out. As I scrambled to get up, she kept yelling about her money and how she was out of whiskey and I had better own up to stealing the money from her. The driver shut the door and I slunk down the aisle to the back of the bus as every kid stared at me. Mom wailed at the bus, "I want my money!"

I walked to school for the rest of the year.

Ten

A jailer led me to the conference room the next morning. Sheriff Robbie entered with a mug of coffee and a doughnut. He munched and seemed pleased to have me handcuffed to a table in his jail.

"In all the excitement I didn't get a chance to tell you it might be simpler if you just made a statement without a lawyer," said the sheriff.

"I couldn't be more innocent, and I want a lawyer," I answered.

"You got one on the way but I don't believe an innocent man really needs or should want one," the sheriff pressed.

"In this county no one needs a lawyer more than an innocent man," I replied. That sentence shut the sheriff up and he stomped away, sputtering something about me being a Yankee in disguise, whatever the hell that meant. Greg walked in with his briefcase and two cups of coffee. He pulled a Krispy Kreme bag out of the briefcase and put two jelly doughnuts in front of me.

"I know the food here stinks and this may be the only time you see something good today. Lunette is putting money on your books right now so you can get snacks at the canteen," said Greg.

"You must think I'm going to be here awhile. What about bail?" I asked.

"I've burned a lifetime of favors this morning. We have a bail hearing tomorrow morning but it's in front of Judge Casey," Greg grimaced.

"That doesn't sound promising."

"He's unpredictable."

"What does that mean?"

"It means he doesn't know what he's going to do until he does it, and then he can't explain what he did or why he did it," Greg offered.

"I shouldn't even be in here. Doesn't anyone understand that?"

"Yeah, me, Lunette, Heather and maybe three others I haven't met."

"Greg, how much is this going to cost?"

"I normally charge four hundred an hour but I am doing this for half. And I am capping this at a hundred billable hours. After that we'll figure something out,"

"It would be cheaper for me to plead guilty," I suggested.

"No, it wouldn't. They want to charge you for the costs of the 'hostage crisis' at the Mossy Head General Store. The sheriff and the county have pegged that little episode at fifty thousand dollars. You do not want to plead guilty to anything," Greg countered.

"There wasn't a hostage, unless you count the dead opossum."

"You know that dead opossum is all over the internet. Somebody has even set up a Facebook page for it. These are strange times."

"Right now, I'd be happier if I were that opossum."

Somebody knocked on the door and Greg cracked it open. I heard "state psychologist" and "evaluation" before Greg held up his hand and spoke briefly.

"Phil, I need a minute in the hallway and I'll be back." He shut the door.

The steaming cup of coffee and two donuts taunted me, as my hands were shackled to the table. I nudged the coffee cup to one side and managed to hold the donuts to the table as I ate each one using my chin for leverage. When Greg stepped back in, he asked a deputy to unshackle me so I could drink the coffee and dab my face with napkins.

"Celebrity has some advantages. The state sent their number one forensic psychologist from Tallahassee over this morning. He asked me if he could interview you and Williemaye together. How do you feel about that?

"Why am I seeing a psychologist?"

"TV coverage brings out a lot of lookie-loos, even official ones. I think he wants a piece of this for his resume or just bragging rights at his next conference. He burned a favor to get this one."

"How does that help me?"

"He could help if he were to testify that Williemaye is a nut case drunk and your only crime is that you are a son who made the mistake of visiting his mother on the day she chose to rob a church."

"So how could this go wrong?"

"Talking too much, explaining too much. Keep your answers very simple, say yes and no as much as possible. If you're not sure, talk to me. If I grab your arm, stop. That means this isn't going the way we need it to go."

"What about Mom?"

"We're counting on her to make it obvious that you are innocent," Greg offered.

We went to a conference room that featured large mirrors covering three walls. I sensed we had an audience. Greg leaned toward me and whispered, "They're going to videotape this meeting. Remember, simple answers. And do not interrupt Williemaye."

Mom sauntered in wearing a bright orange jail smock. She seemed serene, which struck me as weird. She should've had a hangover that would stop a bull elephant in his tracks, and her standard treatment for hangovers was another bottle. Okaloosa County Jail in Crestview wasn't famous for tolerating jailhouse hooch or contraband bottles, so Mom should've been wild for a drink. Instead she looked like an old middle-class retired lady who had been relaxing at a day spa. Like I said—weird.

The state psychologist sat in an upholstered office chair that had wheels. He looked to be in his fifties. He sported a goatee, rimless glasses, and a mustache manicured like it belonged in a barber's textbook. He didn't have much hair but what he did have was greased down. He wore a badge with his name and title emblazoned in bold, black letters that someone must have borrowed from an ophthalmologist's eye chart. A much younger woman appeared to be his assistant. They whispered back and forth several times. She had short hair, no makeup, and never looked anyone in the eye. She sat away from the table and lost herself in a tablet. Mom ignored her but locked on to the psychologist like a missile on its target.

"You the smart sonofabitch they done sent to see if all my screws are properly tightened?" asked Mom innocently.

He ignored her. Shuffled some papers then looked at me with a smile that had all the warmth of an ice cube. "I'd like to talk to Mr. Phil Oglesby first."

"Then why the hell am I here?" Mom complained. That was when the psychologist made his mistake. He answered her question.

"Because I want to interview you and your son together so I can properly assess your interaction," he responded.

"Well, properly assess this. I know three things about you. You like to know what they are?"

"I do not care what you think you may or may not know about me," the psychologist replied.

"I bet you'll care before this is over with." Mom's smile made my blood freeze. This guy was in over his head and didn't know it.

"Are you sure you don't want an attorney present during this interview?" the psychologist asked.

"You got a college degree?" Mom fired.

The psychologist beamed with pride. "I have four degrees."

"Ain't done you no good. You don't seem to understand first-grade English. I said no once, and I shouldn't have to repeat myself in a room this butthole small."

"Then I'd like to start on core issues. Mrs. Oglesby, do you take drugs?"

"You a medical doctor?"

"No, I have a doctorate in criminal psychology," he answered.

"Police put you up to that question?" Mom asked.

"I need to understand your frame of mind, and that question has great bearing on your frame of mind."

"My frame of mind ain't nobody's business!"

"We need to know why you committed this crime." He tapped away on his iPad. "Once again, do you take drugs?"

"I take aspirin once a day, and I take blood pressure pills when I can afford the co-pay."

"Do you take illegal drugs?"

"I would not waste a friggin' dime on illegal drugs, not when there's a bottle of bourbon around," she countered

"Is there some reason you hate this church where this incident allegedly occurred?"

"I don't particularly hate churches," Mom replied.

"Then why did you rob this one?"

"They was advertising a million-dollar Mother's Day offering. Seemed to me they'd have some extra to spare. I don't think God needs that much cash to get along." The psychologist tapped away on his tablet.

"What the hell are you writing about me?"

"Just my notes. I hope you will answer this for me. Do you drink?"

"Like a fish," Mom confirmed.

"How early in the day do you take your first drink?"

"You some kinda moron? I told you I drink. That means I drink in the morning, I drink in the afternoon, and I damn well drink at night. You're just plain dumbass stupid."

"Mrs. Oglesby, I do not care what you think about me."

"You don't care what I think? Well, let me tell you anyway. First of all, you ain't had a woman for at least six months. You looked at my old, saggy knockers when I walked in, and the muscles in your jaw line tightened when I sat down. You like 'em a lot older, don't you? Because they tend to be more grateful than the others who might have a choice besides screwing a stuck up, frozen dick like you. I bet you need a pound of Viagra to have an erection that lasts longer than a minute. And I know something else. Your momma hated your guts, your daddy left her for someone who wasn't a frigid bitch, and you had your first screw in college with someone old enough to be an aunt, probably some old whore so past her prime she paid you," Mom yelled.

The psychologist exploded like a Roman candle. He bounced his chair off the wall as he rocketed from his seat and tossed his cup of coffee into the trash, where it missed the trash can and splashed on the floor. He glared at Mom, and she took another jab before he could exit.

"I bet you been married more times that Zsa Zsa damn Gabor!"

He slammed the door as he left, and his mousey assistant picked up his tablet, his briefcase, and several folders. She looked at Greg. "We may still need to interview your client," she mumbled.

"Y'all tired of me already? You people ain't got much stickin' power do you," Mom sneered.

"You were very rude to a very good man," the assistant defended her boss.

"Good man? He ain't even good enough to be a good idiot," Mom continued her attack. The assistant left.

Greg told me later that the state psychologist drove back to Tallahassee without saying a word to anyone in Crestview. His assistant stayed behind to request the digital recordings of the meeting and to explain that he would send a report in a week or two. He never sent a full report, only a fragment that didn't help the prosecutor at all. Greg also learned that the state psychologist had been married and divorced six times, and when he interviewed Mom he was in the middle of his seventh divorce from a woman twenty years his senior.

"How in the hell did she know that about him?" Greg asked me later.

"She has a gift," I grinned.

Eleven

The jailer took me to a new cell, one with bunkmates. Five of them. Three were playing cards at one set of bunks and the other two were watching TV. No one noticed me. I stood inside the cell and felt the floor rise up and slap me in the face. I woke up with blood in my mouth and inmates crowded around me.

"Somebody think we oughta call a guard?" asked one.

"What for? He ain't bleeding that much," said another.

I tried to sit up, and strong hands steadied me and took me to a bunk. A bearded face gazed into mine. His face was a kaleidoscope of tattoos and scars, and he wore skull-and-crossbones earrings in both ears. He smiled. "You the one they arrested with his momma for robbin' that church on Sunday, ain'tcha?"

"I'm that lucky guy alright," I agreed while blood dripped from my mouth.

"I admire someone who can do something different. Never thought to rob one of those big churches. I can see now that they's a lot like a bank but without no guards, no vaults, and a lot of loose cash, all of it unmarked. How'd you come up with the idea?" he asked.

"I didn't. My mom did the robbing. The mistake I made was to pick her up," I answered.

A voice behind the biker in front of me interjected, "The Good Book says to honor thy father and mother. You done that when you picked her up."

The guy in front of me shooed his interjector away. "Larry, you always quotin' the Bible but it ain't kept your ass out of jail. You still in here with me."

"I'm in here with you because you's my brother, and we got a right bad habit of drinkin' on pay day and bustin' up a bar. You got us in here when you pissed on that deputy's car in front of the Tropical Palm Lounge," Larry replied.

"And you got us in here because you was so drunk you thought the deputy was Uncle Robert and kept telling him he owed us money," he replied.

My head cleared, and I offered my hand to the man in front of me. "Phil Oglesby."

His hand engulfed mine like a catcher's mitt holding a kitten's paw. "I'm Ernie and that's my brother, Larry. That's Randy over there, and them's his poker buddies, Slim and Leo." They grunted and kept playing poker.

"How much money did your momma get outta that church?" asked Larry.

"I'm not sure. I do remember that she had a shopping bag full of cash. Told me she'd—" Ernie slapped his hand over my lips and whispered into my ear that the jail records everything.

Ernie turned to Larry. "Hey bro, what's the first rule in jail?"

Larry hung his head as he answered, "Don't talk about no crimes."

"And what about questions?" asked Ernie.

"Don't ask no questions," muttered Larry while staring at the floor.

"It's the best advice I can give you, Phil, and we all need to follow it," Ernie nodded at his brother. "And you just broke those rules somethin' awful, Larry. And Lord knows you should know 'em by heart by now."

"I'm powerful sorry about it but this man's a celebrity. We all saw him on CNN and all them other channels so it ain't hardly a secret what he was arrested about with his momma." Larry walked to a corner of the large cell and gazed out the small, barred window near the high ceiling. "Phil, I bet you get interviewed a lot when you get outta here. Could you mention me and Ernie? I ain't never been famous and it would make me feel powerful special if you said my name on TV."

"I don't think I'm likely to be on the Today Show anytime soon," I responded.

"I bet you are, and sooner than later," Ernie said with a grin.

A deputy knocked on the door and opened a slot. "Oglesby, your wife's here to see you with your lawyer." I threw some water from the small sink on my face and began to walk out. Ernie motioned to me and whispered, "Be carerful. They bug those meetins with relatives. That's why me and Larry is in here."

"Thanks for the warning," I whispered.

Heather met me at the door to the conference room and hugged me. Greg excused himself for a few minutes.

"I wish I'd never asked you—"

"You couldn't have known," I comforted her.

"I forced you to come. This happened because of me," she said, wiping her eyes.

"This happened because Williemaye is my mom," I answered.

"They have to let you out. Don't they understand?"

"I think the only person with any sense around here is Dwayne, but he's a bit outnumbered. If it were up to the sheriff, I would already be hanging from a rope in Mossy Head."

"Right now I'd like to string him up," Heather blurted between clinched teeth.

"The last sheriff is in jail from what Greg told me, so there is still hope that this sheriff won't make it long either," I said without a smile. Heather kissed me as if we were on the date eleven years earlier when I had proposed and she had answered with a kiss that lasted so long we both ran out of breath.

Greg interrupted, "Sorry to stop the reunion but we have a bail hearing in less than an hour. We've got to talk." Heather sat by my side as Greg asked questions, wrote on a legal pad, and called his office several times. He went over the timeline with me and asked Heather questions about her planning the trip without my knowledge. Then the questions turned to Mom's actions.

"When did you first suspect she might have committed a crime?" asked Greg.

"When I saw the damn checks she tossed on the floor were made out to Grace Chapel."

"Did you do anything that might lead anyone to believe you helped her in any way carry out this robbery?" Greg asked. My mind raced down the chain of events and stopped at something Dwayne had said.

"To put it as elegantly as I know how, I didn't do shit. All I did was pick her up from church," I protested.

"Helping after the fact makes you an accessory. It means we have to prove beyond a reasonable doubt that you were unaware something criminal had happened."

"Doesn't the prosecutor have to prove that?" asked Heather.

"No, in this part of the South they tend to reverse the law on that point," Greg said without a bit of irony.

An hour later I sat in court with Greg. Heather sat just behind us with only a railing between us. She kept her hand on my shoulder. Mom walked in with a woman I presumed to be her public defender, a young, petite African American woman wearing a black pantsuit.

"Williemaye has a good lawyer," Greg wrote on a legal pad in front of me. He whispered into my ear, "That's Kaneisha Tompkins, she's not a public defender and she isn't cheap. Something's going on here."

Mom's lawyer sat next to my mom at the far end of the table. I glanced over my shoulder at the cameras and news crews spilling over the back rows and overflow seats. Reporter Phyllis had the prime spot near the center of the melee. She made eye contact with me and waved, then gestured to her camera operator to focus on me. I turned around. Mom didn't.

Mom stood up, scanned the scene, and announced to the whole courtroom in her booming voice, "Ain't seen this many vultures in one place in my life. Can't you assholes find a greasy car wreck with some decapitated person hanging out of it instead of nosing into my business?" The courtroom tittered with laughs. Mom fired another round. "When I get outta here I'm gonna put my foot up somebody's anus for laughing at me," she insisted. That produced a roar. Her attorney and a bailiff said something to her that stopped her immediately. I had never seen anyone stop Mom once she began a tirade. I heard later that the bailiff promised to bind and gag her if she didn't shut up, but it would have been better for him to let Mom talk herself into being bound and gagged.

Greg leaned over and said to me, "Brace yourself."

"For what?" I asked.

"You'll see," he replied.

Judge Casey entered. He appeared unsteady on his feet, and his bailiff helped him ease his tall, lanky frame into the high-backed chair. The judge motioned for the bailiff, who whispered something no one could hear but everyone heard Casey say, "Can you help me with these damn hearing things?" A split second later his hearing aids squealed as the bailiff adjusted one and then the other. It took several minutes for Judge Casey to be satisfied with the result. He banged everyone to silence with his gavel.

"We have a hearing here for some sort of crime somebody did on Sunday? Or was it Saturday? Mr. Prosecutor, do you know what's going on?" Casey looked straight at Greg.

"Sorry your honor, I'm Greg Polis, defense attorney for one of the defendants."

"Well, damn it all, do you know who you're defending and why?"

"Yes Your Honor, I represent Mr. Phil Oglesby."

"Mr. Oakleaflessly, I sure hope you're innocent because I hate guilty people something fierce. Mr. Prosecutor, would you like to say something about this hearing?" asked the judge.

Clancy Wilkes, the prosecutor, sported a tan, a clean shaven face, and a smile he borrowed from a wolf. "Your Honor, the people charge Williemaye Oglesby with one count of armed robbery, one count of resisting arrest, use of a gun in the commission of a felony, conspiracy, and creating a dangerous situation that led to a standoff at the Mossy Head General Store. We are also charging her son, Phillip Oglesby, with conspiracy to commit this robbery, aiding and abetting the robbery, and crossing state lines to commit a felony. We request bail, if you choose to make that available, in the amount of one million dollars each."

"Mr. Prosecutor, that's a lot of trouble for a jury to decide. Are you sure you need more than one defendant? Two always makes it harder for me to keep things straight," said Judge Casey.

Kaneisha stood and spoke. "I represent Mrs. Williemaye Oglesby, who pleads innocent and request that, due to her advanced age and health issues, she be released on her own recognizance. She has deep ties to this community and does not represent a flight risk. Furthermore, she has no prior convictions." Judge Casey squinted at Mom. She squinted back.

"Do we know each other from somewhere? Seems I've heard your name before," the judge commented.

Kaneisha talked to Mom for a moment and answered, "Mrs. Oglesby doesn't recall ever meeting you before, Your Honor."

Casey wrote a note on the paperwork in front of him and replied, "We got no business keeping Southern women who are senior citizens in jail. I'm inclined to grant release on recognizance."

The prosecutor sprang to his feet. "Your Honor, this Southern woman is charged with armed robbery. She is a danger to the public in this community."

"I don't think so. She looks like my Aunt Malone, God rest her soul. You're even a little prettier," said the judge.

"Your Honor, she robbed a church!" said Clancy. The judge tapped one of his ears and the hearing aid screeched.

"She robbed a what?" asked Casey.

"A church, here in Crestview, on Mother's Day!" Clancy emphasized every syllable. Casey pulled out both hearing aids and tinkered with them. When he put them back into his ears, Greg rose and tried to help my case.

"Your Honor, my client pleads innocent. Phil is Mrs. Oglesby's son, and all he did was pick her up from church on Sunday."

"Well, I can't see how that can be against the law," said Casey. "Unless he hit somebody with the car he was driving," he added. "Did you hit somebody on Sunday, Mr. Oglesby?"

Greg put his hand over my mouth and asked to approach the bench. Clancy asked for the same privilege. When they both stood in front of Casey, Heather made a mistake. She leaned over the railing and gave me a peck on the cheek. Casey saw it.

"I do not tolerate kissing in my courtroom. It leads to other things!" Casey bellowed. He couldn't hear the stifled laughter, and he mistook the smiles that spread across the courtroom as approval for his rant. It wasn't.

At the bench, Clancy issued the first challenge. "Your Honor, I must insist on no bail for Mrs. Oglesby. We allege that she used a gun to rob a church."

"She used a church to rob a what?" sputtered the judge.

"She used a gun!" repeated the prosecutor. He shoved a document in front of Casey, who promptly shoved it back. "I can prove this woman committed a violent, heinous crime on Mother's Day!"

"You can make that case easy with Mrs. Oglesby free on her own recognizance," said Casey.

"Your Honor, are you real sure about that?" challenged Clancy.

"Damn sure," answered the judge.

Greg said, "But Your Honor, Phil Oglesby merely picked up his mother from church after services. He had no reason to suspect a crime had been committed."

"Well, he should have known. He let his mother endanger herself at the scene of a robbery," said Casey without a trace of humor.

"Your Honor, my client did not rob anyone," Greg argued.

"That's for me to decide," replied the judge. He took out his hearing aids and motioned for the attorneys to step back. "An elderly member of our community is alleged to have been involved in some sort of robbery this past Sunday. I'm not quite sure I believe that story, so she is free during the course of this trial. As for this other fellow, he may be responsible for all of this. I don't know but I am going to find out. One million dollars bail." He slammed the gavel down.

It was a body slam, a kick in the gut, and a ripped heart at the same time. I went numb. Cameras popped flashes from the back of the courtroom, and Mom seemed happy and unconcerned about me. Greg whispered to Mom's attorney, and her attorney shook her head and shrugged her shoulders. Heather leaned across the railing and cried as she clutched my shoulder. A deputy intercepted her and led me out of the courtroom.

Twelve

Before I was whisked out of the corridor to the jail, a reporter and her camera crew caught up with me.

"Did you expect to be released from jail today?" she asked.

"I was hoping to be," I answered.

"Do you think the judge misunderstood the charges?"

"I don't know what he understood."

Greg pushed the microphone out of my face and stood in front of the camera. "I need some privacy with my client, who has nothing more to say at this time." Greg followed behind me all the way to the jail's conference room.

"I think you caught a break today in court," Greg said as he poured both of us a cup of coffee.

"A million-dollar bail is a break?"

"TV caught the whole thing. He's been getting away with conduct like that for quite a while. It's one thing when it's petty theft or unpaid traffic tickets, but national news showing a West Florida judge like this? I can promise you three things very shortly: He won't be on this case much longer, you are going to get another hearing in front of another judge, and Williemaye better enjoy the hell out of being free because another judge is not going to let her loose a second time." Greg delivered his speech like he was dead ass certain.

"How has Casey gotten away with this for so long?" I asked, bewildered.

"Relatives, friends, cronies, and connections through marriage and money. His wife's family still owns a good piece of the coastal property south of here, used to own all of it. His daddy was a congressman for so long people couldn't remember a time when he wasn't one. He was OK for a long time, but he began to obviously fall apart the last two or three years. Today's the final nail in his coffin," said Greg.

"You sure you got the right coffin? I feel a bit crowded right now." My chest felt like a rhinoceros had decided to take up permanent residence on my diaphragm. I had no confidence in any judge who might replace Casey.

A deputy knocked on the door and let Heather in. She waved her iPad at us and said, "Williemaye is giving a news conference on the courthouse steps!" She set the screen on its tiny stand and we watched together. Mom stood behind a short podium with a dozen microphones in her face. Her attorney stood beside her with a scowl. Momma looked happier than a cat with an open can of sardines.

"How does it feel to be out of jail?" asked one reporter.

"Feels damn fine. Them baloney sandwiches they tried to make me eat were so hard they could be used to replace bricks in a wall."

"What do you think about the judge's million-dollar bail for your son, Phil?"

"I think that judge was mighty nice to me but he was an asshole to my son, not that my son's all that bright."

"What are your plans for the rest of today?" asked a reporter.

"If you or any other of these puke bastards want me to answer another question, you can meet me at the Tropical Palms lounge around the corner. I haven't had a damn drink in two long ass days and I need some refueling."

A dozen reporters shouted questions as Mom walked away with her attorney jabbering away at her. The camera crews paced her along the sidewalk and kept her on screen as she entered the Tropical Palm Lounge and Grill. Heather turned her screen off but Greg reached over and restarted it.

"We need to watch this," he said.

"What in the world for?" Heather puzzled.

"Because she might just make or break our case on live TV," answered Greg.

Greg opened his satchel and handed me a grease-stained paper bag and a can of chilled root beer. I opened the sack and found four pieces of fried chicken with two large buttermilk biscuits.

"Lunette figured you might want something besides the baloney they serve," murmured Greg.

I ate like a man having his last meal, gobbling up the chicken and biscuits between gulps of root beer. I offered some to Heather but she had no appetite. I paid for it later with indigestion but it was worth the price.

A deputy tapped on the door and poked his head in. "How much longer you think this is going to take? We got a shift change in five minutes. I'd like to get Phil back in his cell, makes the paper work a lot easier." Greg reached into his wallet and tossed a twenty at the jailer, who expertly snatched it out of the air. He pocketed the bill. "Take your time. No reason to hurry," said the deputy. He left us alone to watch Mom on CNN.

Mom was inside the bar on a stool surrounded by cameras, lights, microphones, and reporters drooling to ask her questions. The bartender asked her what she wanted. Mom's answer sent a ripple through the room.

"I'm charging a drink for every question I answer so I hope y'all vultures have an assload of questions. I need a bushel or two of drinks to catch up on what I've missed since being inside that butthole jail." A producer slammed a fifty in front of the bartender. Mom eyed it and snarled.

"That ain't even enough to make me wanna sing 'Mary Had a pissant Lamb'!"

Reporters fumbled for wallets and, in mere seconds, a pile of hundred-dollar bills matched Mom's request. "That's more like it. I'd like a Crown Royal to start," said Mom.

A CNN guy fired the first question. "Did you rob that church?"

"I just attended the service and accepted a donation."

"They gave you the money?" asked an incredulous reporter.

Mom gulped down her drink and yelled at the bartender. "I want some Maker's Mark, a double. And all you sober sonsabitches are making me nervous. You need to be drinking with me if you want me to be sociable and put up with your asinine, piss-faced questions." A second bartender took the flood of drink requests, and news crews began what later became known as the "shot glasses heard 'round the world" interview.

"Yeah, those slick bastards at that church piled money into my shopping bag. It was amazing to see how much they had left over after helping me," Mom snickered.

"Could you tell us and our audience exactly what happened inside Grace Chapel so we can understand what you mean by 'helping' you?" asked a reporter.

Mom asked for the most expensive bourbon in the house and waited to answer until the bartender had the thirty-dollar double bourbon in front of her. She slammed it down in one gulp.

"So you want me to start at the beginning and work my way to the end?" Mom gave no hint that she'd knocked down five drinks already.

"That would be perfect," nodded the reporter.

Mom motioned for another drink and held it in her hand, which shook slightly while she talked. "I walked over from my house since my car is broke, and I showed up after they had begun the service. They got themselves one helluva big church. I ain't seen that many folks in one place since going to the Ringling Brothers Circus in Pensacola back in '52."

"What happened when you went inside?" asked another reporter with a drink in his hand.

"They got more ushers than a whorehouse has pimps. I got offered to sit down front, in the middle, and before they let me sit they said I had to let them put a corsage on my worn out ass. Damndest thing I ever saw. You wear a flower to church if you're getting married or they need to bury you. Waste of a blossom to put it on my dress outside my old tits."

"Where did you sit?" asked the CBS reporter.

"I told one of them ushers that I preferred the back row, and when he said I needed to sit down in front, we argued. I told him that if I needed to piss, I wouldn't make it to no bathrooms in time and that I'd leave a yellow streak on that nice carpet they had. He backed off and let me sit in the last pew."

"Then what happened?" asked the reporter from Time magazine.

"They made a basket load of announcements and then asked all the mothers to stand. I stood up with all the other ones, and the lady next to me looked over and asked me if I was new. I told her I hadn't been inside a church in so long that I didn't know how to spell the word. Then the bitch got nosey and wanted to know where my family was, where my husband was, and where my children was."

Mom stopped and ordered another bourbon.

"Those are interesting questions, Mrs. Oglesby. Did you answer her?" asked a reporter.

"Hell no, ain't none of her business but since ya'll are paying for the liquor, I'll enlighten you. My husband left me high and dry back when my son was two damn years old. Ain't heard from that slimy dick since then and don't care to. We had only one son, and he's over there in jail."

"What happened next in the service?" asked a reporter from WKRG.

"Hell, they commenced to singin'. The choir sang some, the congregation sang some, and then this woman gets up and thought she could sing opera. She wailed so loud on her song I would have sworn somebody was twisting her panties into a knot. She hurt my ears with that yelling she called singing. Made me wish I was somewheres else. The preacher announced the offering before the sermon so that they could announce the amount they collected while everyone was still there in the

73

church. He said it was a million-dollar Mother's Day offering and they'd use the money for God's work.They commenced to take up the offering. Must have had two, maybe three dozen ushers marching up and down the aisles with these offering plates as large as the lid to a fifty-gallon garbage can. I saw those plates fill up faster than a rain barrel in a hurricane. They had to get extra plates."

Mom knocked down another drink and scowled when the reporters seemed hesitant to keep up with her. She insisted that everyone have another drink. It began to take a toll. A camera panned, showing that most them were in over their heads. Three slid off stools on camera and several that were standing began to wobble and lost their footing. One sound guy fell after his fifth drink.

"What happened after the offering?" asked a seemingly sober reporter.

"Well, I joined some of the ushers in a back room and collected my money."

"What do you mean by collect?" asked the reporter.

"I mean I got money and left. You deaf?"

"They willingly gave you the money?" asked the reporter.

"They weren't unwilling," responded Mom.

"How did you precisely get these ushers to give you the money?" another reporter persisted.

"I put a gun to the head usher's crotch and told him I'd blow his balls through the wall behind him if he didn't put a bucketload of bills in my shopping bag," Mom crowed.

"So you admit that you robbed the church?" a reporter asked more like a statement than a question.

"You are one dumb bitch. I robbed the church. That precise enough for you? I robbed the church! You hearing me or is there so much petrified turkey shit in your ears?" Mom snarled.

"I am not a bitch, Mrs. Oglesby, and since we are on a live feed, I must ask that you refrain from using profanity," the reporter fired back.

"Refrain from using profanity? I been sittin' in jail with murderers, rapists, and women who make money by not exactly kissing daisies and you want me to refrain from profanity? Kiss my West Florida Panhandle ass!"

Mom gulped down more bourbon and belched. The eruption startled everyone in the room. "That's a good sign. I think I've had enough to sleep for a while. Bartender, you got any change left so I can get a barbeque sandwich to go?"

The bartender checked the cash on the bar. Reporters and regulars had been adding to the pile while Mom wove her tale. Even after paying for all the drinks, the bartender had enough cash to give Mom two sandwiches. Mom glanced at his empty tip jar and said, "I want some bastard to leave the bartender a tip. He's done more honest work here in an hour that all you sonsabitches do in a year."

The bartender leaned over and informed Mom he'd been smart enough to hold back some cash for a tip. "You ain't as dumb a bastard as most people in this room," Mom said. He handed her the bag of sandwiches.

"Aren't you going to tell us more?" asked another reporter.

"What in the hell more is there to tell you, dumb shits?"

"Why did you rob that particular church and not another one?" asked the WEAR reporter.

"I've told you plenty. I got a lot more drinking to do later, and I ain't gonna use up all this credit in one sitting. You buy me some more drinks later this week, I'll answer some more questions." Mom hopped off her stool and left with her sober attorney fuming at her side.

Thirteen

Mom marched out of the bar with barely a hint of a wobble. Camera crews crowded after her. Reporters shouted more questions, but she ignored them until one blocked her way. She gave him the finger and a volley of cursing that a technician in a sound truck had the good sense to cut after the first three words lit the air on fire. Mom raised her profanity to a new level that stunned everyone around her. If the bar interview had been R-rated, her salvos outside the bar were XXX-rated. The reporter who blocked her path learned that, in Mom's opinion, he was a product of unnatural acts involving his mother, several farm animals, and sexual positions not found in the Kama Sutra. Mom's attorney helped her into a car and drove her away.

A deputy knocked on the conference room door and stepped inside. "Y'all need to wrap this up. I need to get your fellow to his cell."

"Give us five more minutes," Greg requested.

Heather leaned her head on my shoulder. "I'm sorry. I never knew she could be like this." Heather spoke with pain in her voice.

"That's why I kept you away from her. Hell, that's why I stayed away." I gave Heather a long embrace.

Greg cleared his throat and said, "I think it helps our case. Helps a lot. Shows how volatile she is. And she has publicly admitted without any reservation that she committed the robbery. I don't think the next judge will let her stay out on recognizance."

"What about Phil?" Heather fretted.

"I can tell you what about me. That little episode in the bar makes me out to be the son of a lunatic, a woman who is belligerent, alcoholic, and dangerous. People are going to think the acorn didn't fall far from the tree, that I'm just as crazy as she is, that I'm just as likely to be a sociopath."

Confidently, Greg said, "Or they could see you as a victim, a son who stayed away for years to avoid what they saw for their own eyes: a person who robbed a church with a gun then used her son as an unwitting accomplice. You went away to college, earned a degree, built a career in engineering, and you live just about as far away as you could get. I don't think you have much to worry about."

"Would you like to trade places with me?" I asked dryly.

"That might help my reputation as an attorney," Greg said with a grin.

The deputy opened the conference-room door, and I offered my hands as he cuffed me. Heather watched in silence and touched my cheek with her hand.

"Mrs. Oglesby, y'all have to stop that. It's against the rules," the deputy informed her. Heather stepped back as the deputy led me away.

Back in the cell, I was a celebrity. My cellmates had watched the CNN coverage in the courtroom and Mom's drink fest with the reporters.

"Your momma is a real lady. I have never heard a woman who could cuss like that. And she can drink. I think she mighta been able to put my granddaddy under the table. You gotta be proud of her," said Randy.

"I'm not proud of the million-dollar bail," I answered.

"I got to agree with you on bail," said Ernie. "That's powerful high for driving a getaway car."

"I didn't know it was a getaway car."

Ernie slapped me on the back. "That's exactly the truth. You didn't know!" He winked and flashed me a smile that was missing three front teeth.

"My favorite part was when she told 'em to kiss her West Florida Panhandle ass. That is special. I am going to write it down so I can remember it," Randy announced with glee.

The electronic lock on the cell door clanged, and an older African American man with short grey hair stepped inside. He looked at all of us. Randy and Ernie crowded around him and shook hands before bringing him over to me.

"This is Phil, he's new. Phil, this is Leviticus Jones," Ernie introduced them.

I offered my hand and Leviticus shook it. His callused palm felt like a rock. He could have crushed my hand like a peanut shell.

"You get the rollout bed, Leviticus," Randy pointed to a cot folded up in a corner. Leviticus folded it down near the far wall and surveyed the group.

"Ain't none of y'all learned nothing since the last time we was all in here?" Leviticus asked.

The dealer in the poker group raised his head and held up his cards. "I've learned how to win enough cigarettes from these hound dogs so I don't have to buy any in the canteen," he said with a sly smile. His buddies sputtered several snatches of Spanish and kept on playing.

"Ernie, what about you and your brother? Y'all promised me that I wouldn't meet you again unless it was at that fishing spot on the Black Water River," Leviticus scowled.

"I really don't want to talk about it," Ernie sighed.

"I do understand," Leviticus sympathized.

Leviticus lay on his cot and was asleep in one minute. I lay on my bunk with my mind racing. Mom was out on bail and I was in jail. She robbed a church, held off a parking lot full of officers, shot an opossum, winked at a judge, drank the reporters at the Tropical Palm Lounge and Grill unconscious, yet I was in jail even though I have not told a single lie or cursed anyone? I am in jail? That four word sentence—I am in jail, I am in jail—slammed itself around inside my skull until I was sick. I lay on my back and when lights out happened at ten o'clock, those four words had become a dentist's drill penetrating my forehead to the back of my skull. In the dark I made it to the toilet and lost all the chicken and biscuits Lunette had made for me. No one in the cell said a word as I vomited, used the sink, and crawled back to my bunk. I fell asleep listening to someone moaning in a cell down the corridor, a few doors clanking open and close, and a guard's footsteps hurrying away.

Ernie tapped on my chin at three o'clock in the morning. He held his fingers to his lips, leaned down and whispered, "We want to bust you out." He tugged me off my cot. Larry handed what looked like a flash drive with exposed leads to Ernie, who attached the leads to an exposed screw on the inside of the door. The drive's LED glowed and the door slid open. Ernie slithered out first, followed by me then Larry. Ernie used the flash drive again, and the door closed behind us. The corridor was dimly lit and I thought I was dreaming. No one could open an electronic cell door like that outside of Tom Cruise in a *Mission Impossible* script.

I kept quiet as we walked past cells of sleeping men to reach the door that led to the outside corridor. Ernie peered through the glass window in the door and invited me to look. Since it was only a dream, I took a look. A young guard sat asleep at his station in front of a small flat-screen TV showing an infomercial offering instant wealth to anyone willing to buy a $99.95 real estate course. The guard's monitor showed us at the door outside his station. Ernie used the flash drive again and we crept past the sleeping guard.

Ernie opened a janitor's closet at the end of the corridor. We crawled inside, and Larry shut the door behind us. It looked like this had been part of the older jail that had not been remodeled. Ernie pointed to a door at the back of the closet. It had a black, steel padlock. Larry felt across a shelf above our heads, found a key, and unlocked the door.

"This is the way home," Ernie pointed to the door.

We stepped outside under a sky full of stars and into the cicadas' singing. We were in a courtyard with picnic tables and folded umbrellas. A large concrete slab reached from the wall behind us to the chainlink fence twenty feet away. The outside did not smell like a dream; the humidity-loving plants filled the air with an unmistakable scent that washed over me from head to toe. The mosquitoes that bit me drew blood that didn't look imaginary as I smashed them with my hand.

"I thought I was in a dream," I said to Ernie and Larry.

"This ain't no dream. We planned this one before we even got in here," Larry bragged.

"Did you make that thing that opens the doors?" I asked.

"We really don't want to talk about it. Better that you don't know," Ernie evaded.

"What now?" I asked, stunned and fearful.

"Our posse's gonna be here in about a minute and we're headed for the Okefenokee Swamp. Nobody ain't ever gonna find you there," answered Larry.

"I've never lived in a swamp," I said without enthusiasm.

"Think of it as adventure camping. Like on TV," Larry suggested.

"Just don't step on the water moccasins. They don't like it," smiled Ernie.

I heard a distant rumble of motorcycles. This wasn't a dream. Ernie and Larry were escaping and wanted me to escape with them. I hadn't done anything wrong. I didn't belong in jail but if I escaped, that made me guilty of a crime. I didn't want to go but I didn't want to stay. The motorcycle rumble got closer.

Ernie looked at me with concern, "You're the man with a million-dollar bail. It's up to you."

Five motorcycles pulled up outside the fence. Two men in leathers ran to the fence and with deliberate speed cut an opening with bolt cutters.

"I really appreciate what you are trying to do, but I need to face this."

"Can we trust you to keep your mouth shut about how we did this?" asked Ernie.

"You can trust me," I replied. I shook his hand and Larry's.

Mother's Day

Ernie handed me the key to the door and the flash drive that was a lot more than a flash drive.

Fourteen

I stood outside under the stars listening to the motorcycles' rumble grow faint until the cicadas and crickets were the only sound. I went back inside, closed the door, and replaced the padlock, leaving the key on the top shelf. I could barely reach. I knew someone could find me at any moment and realized that I might have been a lot smarter at this moment to be sitting on the back of Harley headed for a swamp than trying to make my way unnoticed back to a jail cell. I stepped out of the janitor's closet, and the infomercial hawking real estate illusions reminded me that a sleeping guard thirty feet away held my life in his hands.

My heart stopped when I realized he was not at his station.

Was he waiting for me on the other side of the door? Was he making a count, about to discover that three men were missing? Was he in the bathroom? Should I turn around and escape through the hole in the fence?

I stayed with my plan. I touched the flash drive leads to the door, the LED glowed, the door opened, and I stepped into the corridor. No guard. This miracle couldn't last much longer so I closed the door and hurried down the hall. I stood in front of the cell door with shaky hands as I tried to use the flash drive. It dropped and skidded across the hallway and lay precariously on a drain grate in the floor. If I made a mistake, it would tumble into a place I could not reach and the morning shift would find me outside my cell in the locked corridor. I began to imagine the questions they would ask and the consequences of my silence. I wanted back in the cell as much as I'd ever wanted anything in my life. I took a deep breath and knelt by the drain. My hand shook again as I reached for the flash drive. I pulled back and prayed for a miracle. I imagined myself in the woods, away from Mom and the waking nightmare that had been my life, and with a hand that did not tremble, I picked up the drive from the drain grate.

Inside the cell no one stirred as I slipped inside. I settled on my bunk with a relief that felt like a cool breeze on a hot day.

"Best get rid of that thing," whispered Leviticus from his cot as he pointed to the toilet. Before flushing the drive, I offered it to him. He refused it.

Morning cell count started at 4:45 a. m. The guard that prisoners sarcastically named Mr. Happy glanced into our cell, tapped on the door, and stood on the concrete floor to check off each name on his list. He barked, "Count confirmed, breakfast in twenty minutes." He didn't look up at first as he began the count. He started with me. "Oglesby?"

I answered as expected, "Present in the cell."

"Jones?"

"Present in the cell," Leviticus boomed.

"Sikes, Ernie?" Silence. "Ernie, I ain't got time for no foolishness. Get off your ass!" Mr. Happy wasn't happy. He looked through the window in the door, then opened the cell and ran to the bunks. He touched the bedding, confusion washing over his face. He quickly rattled off the remaining names.

"Parlier?"

"Present in the cell, señor," answered Randy.

"Nunes?"

"Present in the cell."

"Prescott?"

"Present in the cell."

"Sikes, Larry?"

Mr. Happy leaned out into the corridor and spoke on his two-way handset. "We got a situation here in cell twelve. I'm missing two prisoners." He paused and listened to whoever was on the other end of the conversation. "Yes, it's the Sikes brothers again," he responded. I expected to be hustled out of the cell and questioned. I expected a lot of shouting and screaming. I imagined myself being put on a chain gang for merely knowing about the escape. None of that happened. The jailers tossed the room while we ate breakfast. Leviticus Jones had a conversation with a jail supervisor an hour later. No one seemed to care very much. When Leviticus came back to the cell, his look told me two things: no one suspected me of anything, and I should not say a word to anyone, including Leviticus.

But as I sat on my bunk and pondered the situation, I began to second-guess my decision not to escape. I could be a free man riding on the back of a motorcycle, drinking beer and listening to Ernie and Larry spin tales about their insane, lost lives. But I realized escaping would have also been a prison. It seemed I couldn't win.

Leviticus caught my eye and seemed to look into my soul. He motioned me over to the card game he was winning. "Cash me out," he said to Randy, who gave him two packs of cigarettes. "I don't usually talk much in here but I think you need to hear some things. The Good Book says to honor your mother and your father all the days of your life that it may be well with your soul.

When you picked up your momma from church, you honored that commandment."

"I wish I had never come down here," I mumbled.

"But you did and now you get to live a different life."

"I don't care for it very much," I admitted.

"I've found out that what I do or don't care for ain't got much to do with what happens," responded Leviticus.

"Larry said it wasn't a good idea to talk very much in the cell. Isn't this risky?" I asked.

"Larry likes to impress new folks like you with advice. The biggest problem inside is a man who uses what someone tells him to get a plea deal. A snitch. Those folks tend to die suddenly."

"I don't plan on being a snitch," I denied.

"I wouldn't be talkin' to you if I thought you was," Leviticus grinned. He didn't say another word for a long minute. "Have you forgiven your momma?"

"Forgiven her for what?" I asked, surprised.

"Sittin' here in this jail cell for one thing," Leviticus proclaimed.

"No, I haven't forgiven her."

"You're making a powerful big mistake. I don't care what she done to you. You gotta forgive her," decreed Leviticus.

A moment later Deputy Dwayne stopped by to see how I was doing. . . Dwayne took me out of the cell to a holding area near his desk. When another jailer insisted I wear shackles while out of the cell, Dwayne gave the man a withering stare . He also broke another rule when he handed me a sausage biscuit and poured me a cup of coffee. Jail inmates were not fed lunch.

"Don't worry about the Sikes brothers. This ain't the first time they've left a cell prematurely. They had an uncle worked in this jail for forty years. We all knew him and he doted on those two like they was his own kids. He was a bachelor and word was he made some money on the side bootleggin' and that Ernie and Larry pretty much ran that business for him. He moved in with them when he retired seven, eight years ago. Cancer and diabetes got him back in 2008. His funeral at the Seminole Baptist Church was standing room only. The boys got arrested two months later and were sentenced to thirty days. They must've got bored in here because they left with two weeks to go. Seems like they replayed some history last night. We've had more trouble keeping those two in jail than keeping cookies in a cookie jar. It's like they had keys to the damn place," Dwayne smiled at me as he said that. I trusted Dwayne but I also remembered Leviticus's advice.

"I wish I had a key out of here."

"I saw Williemaye's drinking contest at Tropical Palms on TV. She admitted guilt plain as day. And the sheriff is fuming because she's out without bail," Dwayne chuckled.

"Does he honestly think I belong in here?"

"I don't know that Robbie thinks very much at all. His wife does most of the thinking in that family, and the only time anyone pays much attention to him is when he's on the phone in his office or down at the courthouse," Dwayne supplied.

"Where does that leave me?"

"Phil, I can tell you this much. Tallahassee has pulled that judge off your case and off the bench. I heard that this morning. And it is permanent. You're getting a new bail hearing tomorrow morning, first thing. The judge is a man named Hightower. I've never heard of him but maybe your lawyer knows something about him. Lawyers and judges in these parts are thicker than molasses kept in a freezer."

Dwayne let me bring my coffee along on the short walk back to the cell. Another guard stopped us and told me I had an urgent meeting with Greg in the conference room. Thanks to Dwayne, I thought I knew what it was about. I was dead wrong.

Fifteen

Breakfast that morning was a special one, overcooked eggs on top of cold grits. The biscuit was also special; the weevils baked inside were called "protein" by the inmates. I had given my breakfast to Leviticus, who shared it out with the others. When I walked into the conference room, Greg handed me a basket, another meal from Lunette. I wolfed down Lunette's peach cobbler and chased it down with hot, fresh coffee.

"We caught a big break this morning," Greg announced.

"Hightower," I sputtered the name between bites of cobbler crumbs.

"Word does travel fast in jail. Yeah, and it's mostly good. A deputy is bringing your civvies for you to wear to court in about fifteen minutes. We have another bail hearing. Hightower is allowing limited press coverage. Only local stations and one national, CNN."

"What's the good part?" I asked after gulping some coffee.

"Casey is off the bench for good. That little comedy in the courtroom embarrassed the shit out of the state judiciary. More than one person put it on YouTube, and it has over ten million hits. I thought they would work fast but even this is exceptional. There's a lot of stink on the county right now and they'd like to get rid of it," Greg shook his head.

"Does that mean they're gonna go ahead and shoot me?"

"Right now they wish they'd never seen you or Williemaye. The State Attorney General called me last night. That's a first for me. She told me they want you out of jail on recognizance pending more discussion."

"So I get out today?" I asked with disbelief.

"Yes, I think Hightower has two goals today, release you and lock up Williemaye."

"So my bail is going away and Mom is going to jail?"

"That's about the size of it," Greg shrugged.

"Why do they want to lock her up again?"

"Her performance at the Tropical Palm pretty much proved that she was guilty and extended more than a gallon of reasonable doubt about you. With her on the outside, the publicity is scalding a lot of people. They do not know what she's going to say next," Greg contemplated.

"I don't even think she knows what she's going to say next."

A deputy knocked on the door and handed Greg my sports coat and the rest of my clothes that were wrinkled all to hell. I started to dress, but Greg pulled a garment bag off a chair and handed it to me. It held a pressed shirt, a boring tie, clean socks and underwear, and pants that lacked the dirt stains of my unwashed trousers. When we entered the courtroom, Greg let me pause at the next to last row for a quick embrace with Heather.

Ten minutes later I stood in court at Greg's side as Judge Hightower entered. While Judge Casey had looked like a fat, old rag doll, Hightower had the ramrod straight back of a Marine Corps Drill Instructor. His face looked like someone had carved it out of the marble image of a first-century Roman senator, stern, silent, and determined. When Mom met him, it would be a battle of the ages. A rigorous, humorless jurist versus an emotional great white shark. I placed all bets on Mom.

Hightower looked at the back of the court and counted the news crews. He motioned for the bailiff to come forward and said, "I am only allowing WEAR, WKRG, and CNN to this hearing. I see six crews—too crowded and unsafe for this old judge to tolerate—so I am directing my bailiff, Mr. Sammy Bass, to escort the rest of you outside while we do our business this morning."

One crew refused to budge. The bailiff called over two more deputies and whispered something to the reporter that led to an immediate withdrawal. Urban legend said the deputies planned to pepper spray them but it was a lot simpler. They were going to Taser them if they didn't leave. With inaudible grumbles they made their way to the double doors at the back of the court room. Their surge came to a halt when Mom's voice boomed into the courtroom from the hallway.

"I don't give a friggin' frog's fart who they are. Get out of my damn way you dumb, cross-eyed bastards!" Mom's greeting to the media produced a gentle cascade of laughter and grins in the courtroom.

I glanced at Hightower. Even he couldn't resist a Mona Lisa smile, but he covered it up quickly. Kaneisha, Mom's lawyer, rushed to her side to shush Mom, who wasn't buying the advice. "I been in this damn place before and that last judge was dumber than dried cat shit. What makes this one so special?"

Judge Hightower answered her question. "What makes me so special is that I am a retired Florida Supreme Court Justice. I was asked to accept this temporary appointment by the Florida's governor. I expect you to respect this court."

Mom measured him from the defense table. We sat less than a yard apart. She glared at him but retreated into herself. Judge Hightower took her silence as acquiescence. I knew better. I had seen her do this before, pretend to agree only to pounce harder, bite deeper, and shriek louder.

"This is a new bail hearing for Mr. Greg Oglesby and in a related matter, Mrs. Williemaye Oglesby. I'd like to talk to Mr. Oglesby's attorney first, up here," said Hightower.

Judge Hightower waved Greg over to a short conference between the two of them. Prosecutor Clancy scowled and shook his head at me. Judge Hightower looked up in time to catch our little drama, and Hightower stared at Clancy like he was a blowfly on his wife's pecan pie at Thanksgiving dinner.

"Mr. Prosecutor, you will not stare at a defendant in my court. You will not make faces in my court. If you are suffering from piles or indigestion or a heart attack, you wait until you are outside this court room to be visibly uncomfortable. Do you understand me?"

Clancy mumbled, "Yes, Your Honor."

"I said do you understand me?" The judge's question echoed like a cannon shot.

"Yes, Your Honor." Clancy answered in a loud but shaky voice.

"Good. I like that tone much better."

"I have had a chat with Mr. Oglesby's attorney and we have agreed that he is to be released on his own recognizance but he is not to leave the county without the permission of this court. Do you understand this instruction, Mr. Oglesby?"

"Yes, Your Honor. I do."

"Mr. Prosecutor, do you have any objections?" asked Hightower.

"I believe he is a flight risk, Your Honor, and while I do not like to criticize Sheriff Robbie, I want the court to know that two men, cellmates of Mr. Oglesby's, escaped from the jail last night. We suspect Mr. Oglesby may have information pertinent to that escape since he was present in that cell," said Clancy.

His words froze me in my chair. I stopped breathing.

"Mr. Clancy, you can't have it both ways. You tell me this man's a flight risk when he stays in a cell while two others escape from the same cell. You might make a better defense witness than prosecutor in this case. I am noting your objection and am granting Mr. Oglesby release on his own recognizance," Judge Hightower pronounced with a small smile. Greg patted my hand. I started to breathe again.

"On the matter of Mrs. Williemaye Oglesby, I am going to grant the People's request to impose bail and remand to custody. I will, however, entertain remarks from Mrs. Oglesby's attorney before declaring the amount of bail," said the judge.

Kaneisha whispered to Mom then rose to speak to Hightower.

"Your Honor, Mrs. Oglesby does not represent a flight risk. Her car is broken and she has lived in this community since 1952. She has no felony or misdemeanor convictions on her record. I would urge the court to consider her advanced age, her long residence in Crestview, and the eccentric nature of the charges against her as a basis for either recognizance or very low bail."

Hightower took notes while Kaneisha spoke and shuffled a handful of papers. When she finished he looked at Clancy.

"Would you like to add something Mr. Prosecutor?" asked the judge.

"I would not call robbing a house of God on Mother's Day with a .38 caliber revolver eccentric. I would call it a callous disregard for decency, the lives of others, and moral turpitude of the highest order. We're charging her with multiple felonies: armed robbery, terrorism, kidnapping, resisting arrest, and drunk and disorderly conduct. This woman is a danger to everyone around her, and—"

"You shit pile in a suit. The only moral turpitude I see is letting some dumb pecker redneck like you prosecute anyone guilty of anything beyond jay walking. As for being drunk and disorderly, I'll bet a dollar to a turd-load of doughnuts that your Momma had to be wild ass drunk for someone to be desperate enough to stick something inside her that made you—"

A deputy shoved his hand over her mouth. She bit him, and she did not let go. He dragged her to the floor while the court gasped. He stooped over Mom, who had the meat of his thumb and first finger clinched between her jaws. He screamed, a news crew rushed forward to record the mayhem, and Judge Hightower pounded his gavel once. It splintered. A crowd of bailiffs separated Mom from the deputy's bleeding hand. Mom looked like a gleeful vampire and the deputy looked like a gut-shot deer. Mom spit the deputy's blood out of her mouth onto the defense table. She looked as calm as a sailboat on a serene lake.

"That sonofabitch had no business sticking his paw into my mouth," Mom growled.

Hightower had found another gavel. He struck it once and quiet descended. Even Mom shut up.

"Mr. Deputy, did I ask you to stick your hand into Mrs. Oglesby's mouth?" asked the judge.

The deputy shook his head.

"I don't do sign language in my courtroom, deputy. I need an answer the stenographer can use," ordered Hightower.

"No, Your Honor. You didn't ask me to do that."

"I'm glad you understand because such an action implies that I cannot control my courtroom. I do not like such implications, especially on the part of an officer of the law. Everyone in this room understand that? I don't need interventions unless I ask for them. Don't anyone within the sound of my voice make a mistake like that again. Now, Mrs. Oglesby, I suppose your attorney might argue that you responded to an unprovoked assault. And I would make such an argument myself as your attorney. For the record, you may not verbally abuse anyone in this courtroom. That includes the prosecutor. You have a very capable defense attorney in Ms. Tompkins. Let her object for you, otherwise I may have to direct that you may only attend these proceedings via closed-circuit TV, which may limit your ability to fully participate in your defense. Do you understand what I am requesting of you?"

I sucked air. Asking Mom a question was an invitation to a verbal ass kicking, judge or no judge.

Mom sat in her chair with the deputy's blood dripping down her chin. Her lawyer whispered something to her. Mom stared at Hightower who stared back at her. Neither of them blinked. Neither seemed in a hurry. Then she surprised me. "I appreciate you keeping that dumbass deputy out of my mouth. He didn't taste that good," Mom countered.

Hightower squirmed and looked away as he tried to hold himself together. He was clearly fighting the urge to laugh, and his iron will gave him the edge to respond with words that seemed to crawl out from clinched teeth. "I am glad you found his taste disagreeable. I do not want to see cannibalism added to the charges against you."

They smiled at each other. Surprised laughter rippled through the court. The judge scored points with the press, the courtroom audience, and later that evening with late-night comedians. I held my breath, expecting Mom to bitch-slap His Honor all the way back to Tallahassee.

"I ain't never been no cannibal," murmured Mom with emphasis on the last word.

"I am glad we can agree about that. Let's get back to business. Mr. Clancy, would you care to finish your statement without interruptions?" Hightower asked the question while looking pointedly at Mom's attorney. Kaneisha whispered to Mom, while Mom looked at a paler-than-normal Clancy. Without saying a word and without catching his eye, Mom successfully intimidated the District Attorney for the County of Okaloosa.

"I simply wish to repeat my request for no bail, Your Honor," said Clancy without much enthusiasm.

"Noted, Mr. Prosecutor," boomed Hightower, his voice echoing in the court. Hightower scribbled on some more papers then began to read from what had to be a prepared text. "This case is unique in that it involves our religious community, an elderly citizen who has lived most of her life in this town, and a son who grew up in Crestview and has, as best as I can tell, been a model citizen wherever he has lived. Publicity rarely helps a case and often distorts facts beyond recognition. I believe that has happened here. Realizing that the truth has yet to be determined, I am going to extend to Mrs. Oglesby some courtesy. As a matter of judicial fairness, I want to postpone a bail hearing for Mrs. Oglesby pending several matters. One, Mrs. Oglesby needs to stay in our custody for the time being. Two, I want a court-appointed psychiatrist to interview both Mrs. Oglesby and her son tomorrow morning at 8 a.m., sharp. I have instructed Dr. Greene to interview you separately. Don't make any other plans for tomorrow morning, Mr. Oglesby." The judge casually looked my way. "Mrs. Oglesby, you are going to be our guest pending the outcome of the evaluation with our psychiatrist. Your responses will largely decide whether or not I grant bail, and if I do grant bail, the amount of bail I impose. Please cooperate. Three, I believe in freedom of the press and speech. It is what makes this democracy work most of the time and it keeps people honest. Despite requests, I am not issuing a gag order. But—and this is especially true for you, Mr. Oglesby—be very judicious in what you choose to say both in public and private forums about this case and your involvement with it. As for you, Mrs. Oglesby, I do not think your defense was well served by your cocktail party last night. I hope you will not repeat such a performance should this court grant bail at some point in the future. " Judge Hightower flashed a smile at the back of the courtroom at the gaggle of news cameras catching his every word. "Lastly, I know everyone and his momma is talking about this ruckus, but I do not want officers of the court or their relatives or their best friends or their cocker spaniel on 'Good Morning America' offering their wisdom about this. It better not happen."

He alternated glaring stares at both attorneys as he made his statement.

Sixteen

I walked out of court holding hands with Heather. I was free but not really free. Despite the judge's order, news crews blocked the steps with microphones and cameras. They shouted questions like bidders at a final auction for my soul. Greg stood beside us and shouted, "My client is free pending further investigations. It is not in his interests to make any comments at this time."

"Are you guilty of helping your mother rob Grace Chapel?" asked a reporter, ignoring Greg's plea. The reporter, a tall guy wearing a suit and flashing a toothy smile, shoved his microphone at my face. I snapped my head away but not fast enough. He clobbered me in the throat with enough force to knock me to the ground. Heather slapped him so hard it knocked a contact out of his eye and sent the microphone tumbling to the ground.

Cameras caught all of it.

The reporter screamed something about suing Heather. Deputy Dwayne with two other beefy deputies rescued us. We plowed through the crowd to Lunette in a curbside car. Dwayne told me later that he had a brief but pointed talk with the reporter. Told him that it would have been self-defense if Heather had shot him. He also told the reporter that he had given Heather a 9mm pistol with instructions to shoot him next time he so much as brushed against either of us. Dwayne said the reporter mentioned something about the Bill of Rights, and Dwayne explained that he knew what that was but Crestview wasn't Miami or Key West or even Orlando. Most people in these parts had a limited view of what rights people had, especially if the people aggravated someone unnecessarily. The reporter didn't sue and the next time I saw him, he kept his distance.

Heather wanted me to go to the emergency room to get my throat checked, but the news trucks following us convinced me that a simpler solution was best. Lunette stopped at the market, and Greg ran in to buy a bag of ice and Ziploc bags. A baggie of ice kept my throat from swelling. I was able to speak, although only in a whisper at first.

Lunette drove us to the motel where Heather was staying. That was a mistake. Heather had registered under her own name, so the same horde of reporters that had clogged the courthouse steps blocked the entrance to the Holiday Inn Express.

"I'm hungry," said Greg from the front seat. "Let me get us to a good place away from this blockade."

Greg exchanged places with Lunette and blew out of the parking lot before a single satellite news truck could shift gears. He ran three stoplights and took a side street that only locals used. A few minutes later he parked us in a shady grove of trees where it was impossible to see the car from the road. He walked us to a restaurant that I remembered as the Mim's home, an old place built in the thirties and nearly falling down when I graduated from high school. It now had a sign that read: *The Wild Branch*. It was lunch time, and cars filled the gravel parking lot. Inside, Greg said something to the man at the register and he gave us to a table in the far corner of the dining room. Everyone stared a hole into Heather and me. I stared right back. A waiter gave us menus while the staring continued.

"OK, everybody, for the record I am Phil Oglesby and I just got out of jail. My momma is still in jail and I would like to eat a meal without all of you looking like you expect me to be selling crack cocaine." I spoke without raising my voice. A tittering of awkward laughter replaced the stares, and people went back to their food and left us alone with the exception of a few sideways glances. I asked Greg if they had a wine menu.

"No, Brother Phil, we are too close to the Protestant Vatican to drink wine in this place. You'll have to make do with Pepsi or Coke or sweetened ice tea." Greg made the statement without a smile. The food almost made me forget that my throat was sore. The blackened steak that I slowly chewed and swallowed with care, while holding Heather's hand, almost made me forget my predicament.

"What really happened back there in court?" I asked.

"You got out of jail," answered Greg.

"Is he out for good?" Heather inquired.

"I suppose we need to talk about that," Greg conceded.

"So, I'm not in the clear yet?" I asked with my guts in a knot.

Greg looked around at the other diners. The closest table was ten feet away but he had already noticed a few surreptitious smartphone users snapping photos. Greg reached inside his coat for a sheet of paper and scribbled a note to me. I didn't understand his message at first.

The note read: *You need to testify.*

I motioned for Greg's pen. I took it and wrote a question: *Testify about what?*

Williemaye's crime.

I wrote: *I don't understand.*

Greg scribbled furiously for a moment. *You need to be willing to testify for the prosecution.*

"Why do they need me? She admitted her guilt on national television!" I blurted, not caring whether anyone heard me.

"Admission on TV is not admission in court. The prosecutor wants your cooperation. So does Hightower," Greg contributed in a lowered voice.

"What does cooperation mean?" Heather wanted to know.

"It means being a friendly witness for the prosecution against Williemaye," said Greg in a hushed voice.

I felt sick. Mom had used me to help her commit a crime. I was her unwitting getaway driver. The son who had driven her to an out-of-town ATM machine, and on a sheriff's barked command, dumped hundreds of thousands of dollars into a stiff breeze in a Mossy Head parking lot. I had come to Crestview to negotiate a sort of emotional peace treaty with a woman who had embarrassed me throughout my childhood. A mother whose contempt for everyone around her made me spend every moment I could away from my so-called home. A mother who had sucker punched my bride's mother at our wedding. Despite all that, the thought of testifying against her made me sick. And that made me angry with myself.

In a moment, an image of my eight-year-old self flashed through my mind. It was a cold day and I left the house to meet Jimmy, a kid down the street who lived a life I envied. He had two parents who never yelled, a house where the electricity was never turned off, a refrigerator that always had real food and— something I never quite understood—leftovers. Jimmy lived in his own little corner of this heaven. His parents had built him a bunkhouse behind their home, complete with a bedroom, his own TV with an outside antenna, and, most gloriously, a playroom stocked with toys. He was an only child so his parents didn't mind if I showed up to keep him occupied in his separate paradise. I had spent the morning at Jimmy's and finally went home before lunch, disappointed at not being asked to stay and eat but grateful for the milk and peanut butter cookies Jimmy shared earlier. I was crossing the street to get back home when I saw Mom amble out the front door. She staggered to our car, a Ford Pinto with dents on every side from her drunken jaunts. She squinted across the street at me and made a face. She backed the car up so fast she ran up on the neighbor's yard where I was standing. She missed me because I dove out of her way. She rolled down her window, grinning, and her breath frosted as she yelled, "You're a quick little bastard or you'd be dead. Stay out of my way." And she drove off. I didn't go back inside the house. I spent the rest of the day finding bottles to sell to the grocery store, and I made enough to buy a hamburger and fries.

Mother's Day had given me a chance for revenge. I could testify against her in court with all the world watching and help put her away. But it didn't feel right, and I didn't know why.

I had been silent for several minutes while remembering that cold day in January, thirty-one years ago. Most of the diners had left and Heather was stroking my hand, but I hadn't noticed. The server brought a dessert menu and Greg asked me three times if I wanted peach cobbler with ice cream.

"Sorry, I got lost thinking about testifying. Peach cobbler would be great," I answered.

"You don't want to testify?" asked Lunette.

"You don't have to answer her," smiled Greg. "We can talk about it later."

"Something about this bothers me. I haven't done anything wrong. I simply want to board a plane and leave with Heather."

"You can't do that right now," Greg stressed.

"But if I have to testify, that means staying here for months and spending money that Heather and I don't have," I groaned.

"It might not be as long as you think," Greg clarified in a low voice.

"How long is long?" Heather inquired.

"Hightower wants an expedited hearing, a plea bargain from Williemaye, and a ribbon on this little shindig inside of two weeks. From what I've heard, one week would suit him better," answered Greg.

"Then why does Phil need to testify?" Heather puzzled.

"Clancy doesn't want to drop the charges against you unless you're cooperative. Hightower wants a plea deal to be very clean, no untied knots, and leaving you out seems like a large loose string to the court," answered Greg.

"Why do they want to avoid a trial?" I asked with suspicion.

"I don't know if we want the answer to that question," Greg answered.

"I'd like your opinion," I responded. "Why do they want to avoid a trial?"

Greg glanced around our end of the restaurant. All the tables were empty. "I'm going to speculate, Phil, not because I know for sure but because I know that somewhere in my random thoughts there is some version of the truth. First, this mess has generated a lot of publicity and none of it's very good for the powers that be in Crestview. Their friends in Tallahassee don't like it much either. That's one piece of it and probably the biggest one."

"What's the other piece?" Heather interrupted curiously.

"That's the tricky part. I think Grace Chapel is none too happy about this situation."

"Even I get that, they don't like being robbed on a Sunday morning," I agreed.

"No, Brother Phil, you don't get it," Greg said, without a smile.

"Then what's the deal, why don't they want a trial?" I pressed.

"Six years ago, one of their pastors came to me for some legal advice. You might appreciate that such conversations are privileged—I don't share them with the court and the court doesn't ask. And I don't tend to share them with anyone except Lunette and Duke, our dog. "

"So you're about to say something that we shouldn't really hear?" Lunette asked in a hushed voice.

"You've put your finger on exactly the right spot. I'm going to share hypotheticals with you. Remember what those are?"

"*Law & Order* was the only program we watched back in college," answered Heather.

"Imagine that you have a big, successful church. Congregation's busting at the seams, folks driving fifty or sixty miles to be at services on Sunday morning. Four or five years earlier, the church had maybe three hundred members and now it has three thousand. You have some growing pains." Greg paused. Heather locked eyes with him.

"I know the next sentence. The church has a lot of money coming in and they are probably using the same accounting system they used when they had the smaller church," Heather reasoned.

"This hypothetical church didn't have an accounting system," Greg explained. "This hypothetical church had ushers who counted money and kept a system of ledgers for donations, in pencil, not even ink. No computers, no hard drive, and every opportunity for someone to steal them blind."

"Someone stole this hypothetical church blind?" I interjected.

"If you were someone with some responsibility in this church, what would you do to confirm your suspicions?" asked Greg.

"I would use bait cash, marked money, and a remote camera system connected to a hard drive," Heather responded.

"Hypothetically, that's what they did and it worked," Greg confirmed.

"Hypothetically, who stole the money?" I inquired.

"In this hypothetical church, one member was a bank teller, and she was also the modestly paid bookkeeper for the church. Best guess they were able to make after they stopped her activities is that she hypothetically embezzled five hundred thousand dollars," Greg said with a smile.

"How much time did she get, hypothetically?" I probed.

"Not one day. Not even an hour. You've spent more time inside jail than she ever did."

"She stole a half million dollars and got away with it?" Heather looked stunned.

"She was the lead pastor's mother-in-law. It was a might embarrassing, hypothetically."

Seventeen

We walked out of the restaurant into a hail of camera flashes and two news crews with satellite trucks. Someone inside the restaurant had twittered about our lunch and posted photos on Instagram. I realized I had about as much privacy as Lindsey Lohan. A reporter was on me before we walked five feet. He held his microphone to his side and used his crew to block other news crews trying to get a clear view. A loud argument splintered the air as his guys argued with the other guys.

"If you will give me an interview with your attorney present, I will leave you alone. You need to get your side of the story out to the public. I really do want to help you," he pleaded.

"The judge in this case specifically instructed my client to avoid publicity, interviews, and séances. He's not available," Greg reacted immediately.

The scrum followed us to Greg's car. We drove away with cameras trained on us until our car was out of sight. Greg stopped in front of our hotel, where only one satellite TV truck stood vigil near the entrance.

"You like me to run interference with you?" asked Greg

"No. I've got on my big boy pants. We can handle this." We got out of the car and a news crew was on me like white on rice. They were local, WKRG.

"Did you expect to get out of jail today?" asked the reporter guy.

"I didn't know what to expect but right now I'd like to get to my room and rest," I answered.

I took a step and he didn't block my way or follow us inside.

Heather and I held hands as we walked through the lobby to the elevator. We had a room on the fourth floor and she led me to our room. She closed the door and we shared a kiss that lasted an hour.

The phone interrupted. We ignored the call. Five minutes later it rang again. I picked up.

"This had damn well better be the end of the fucking world," I growled.

Greg chuckled on the end of the line. "You have been around Williemaye a little too much."

"Sorry for the rudeness," I muttered.

"Wanted you to know we meet with the court appointed psychiatrist at 8 a.m. Get some rest, kiss Heather, and I'll see you in the morning," said Greg.

"I'm way ahead of you," I replied. I hung up the phone, and Heather resumed the kiss.

Heather fell asleep first. I lay in the king-size bed, staring at the ceiling. Light splashed across the room from the almost closed drapes. I thought for a moment that some crazed photographer had thrown up a ladder and taken a picture of us in bed. Another flash sliced across the room and then, seconds later, the long, rolling boom of a Florida thunderstorm shook the window. Heather didn't budge. Her measured breathing beneath the covers showed she slept while I parted the drapes and sat in the almost comfortable office-style chair at the desk next to the room's picture window. I sat naked watching lightning slash across the sky. The heart of the storm reached the hotel. Sheets of rain pounded the window as thunder bellowed and lightning briefly sliced night into day. Winds blew fronds off the palm trees and several hit the side of the hotel. I slipped out of the chair, into the bed, and embraced Heather who murmured something about good night in her sleep. While the storm passed through, I lay in bed and thought about Ernie and his brother in the distant swamp, swatting mosquitoes, drinking beer, and telling their buddies about the guy arrested for picking his mother up from church. I wondered if they knew that I was out. I doubted it. Not too many cable connections in the Okeefenokee. I thought about Leviticus Jones, Randy, and his buddies. The Okaloosa County Jail had no air conditioning and it was as soundproof as an aluminum can. I imagined the thunderous booms slamming through the cells, waking each man who then had to lie on his thin mattress, his ears ringing from the thunder. Inside the hotel room, the thunder was muffled and the air conditioner added a breathy white noise to the muffled chaos outside. In the morning I would wake up next to Heather and probably shiver in the artificial chill in our room. My cellmates would wake up to a sauna as the sun began to cook the jail.

Heather shook me awake at 6 a.m. I didn't want to get up. And I definitely didn't want to go back to the jail for an interview with a psychiatrist. My mind played a sick version of the '*What If*' game while I showered. What if the shrink decided I was a guilty accomplice? What if the judge had changed his mind and decided that I belonged back inside the cell with Leviticus and the others? What if the prosecutor had convinced the judge that I was a risk? Twenty variations of the What If questions pranced through my skull while I tried to enjoy my first morning shower out of jail. I was trembling when I walked out of the bathroom. Heather held me while I gulped for air.

"You don't need to worry. You haven't done anything," she assured me.

"I keep saying that to myself, but it doesn't seem to help," I replied.

We ate breakfast in the dining room just off the lobby. We were not alone. A few families with small children ate noisily. The kids bickered and shrieked with laughter as one of them dumped chocolate milk down his mother's dress. No one seemed to notice us.

"How long can you stay?" I finally asked Heather.

"Until Sunday, then I've got a meeting I can't miss early Monday."

"We can't afford to keep me in this hotel indefinitely."

"We can afford this week. Then we'll worry about the rest of it as it happens."

I began to disagree but Heather put a buttermilk biscuit with blackberry jam in my mouth and that shut me up.

No one ambushed us outside the hotel. I relaxed during the short drive to the courthouse. Heather decided to park on First Street, a block away from the courthouse steps. We walked holding hands until we reached the sidewalk in front of the building. The scrum of reporters and news trucks dominated the steps and the entrance. We tried walking along the outside of the fray but only made it ten feet before the cameras latched onto us like laser beams. Dwayne and two other deputies rescued us and acted like ice breakers to get us inside the courthouse. We met Greg in a conference room.

"We've got about ten minutes before the new psychiatrist interviews you. I expect this to last an hour. If she asks a question that I don't like, I can object because while this is not for the record, it does have legal weight. The prosecutor will have an assistant DA present, and he or she can take notes. Williemaye's lawyer has asked to be present and I have no objection to that if you don't," Greg informed me.

"It doesn't matter to me."

"Can I be there?" asked Heather.

"I'd rather you wait in the hallway," Greg answered.

"You don't want me there?" Heather sounded hurt.

"I don't know a thing about this psychiatrist. If you're in the room, it adds another element that might lead to an unpredictable question or something that angers you or Phil. Anger isn't our friend. Not in a session like this," answered Greg.

Heather glumly nodded her agreement.

"What do I need to watch out for?" I asked.

"Simply keep your eye on me. If I shake my head, don't answer."

"Won't that make me look uncooperative?"

"It'll make you smart," responded Greg with a grin.

Deputy Dwayne opened the door at eight on the dot. He walked in with a woman I first took as a lost high school student. She went to the head of the conference table and opened her laptop.

"Could you move to this chair?" she indicated the chair next to her.

I moved and realized that this girl with a ponytail and a University of Florida pullover was the psychiatrist. She explained why she wanted me to move as I sat down. "Thank you. I am going to record this interview using the camera in my computer. It helps with the recording to have the subject closer."

The camera port on the back of her laptop aimed toward my face.

"I don't remember agreeing to this," Greg protested.

"Are you objecting?" asked the psychiatrist as Mom's attorney walked in with the assistant DA.

"Yes, I am. Records like this are easy to edit and subject to abuse."

"What are you willing to accept?" asked the psychiatrist.

"Sound, no video," Greg conceded.

The psychiatrist shut her laptop, passed a note to the assistant DA, and waited to begin until Deputy Dwayne entered the room and placed microphones in front of everyone seated at the table.

"Y'all are wired for sound. Let me know when it's over so I can put this gear up for the next party," Dwayne said as he left the room.

"I'm Daphne Greene from the office of the state psychologist. I am here to interview Phil Oglesby and Williemaye Oglesby. She's your mother?" she asked looking at me.

"Williemaye is my mother."

"Have you ever had a psychiatric evaluation?" asked Daphne.

"Never," I replied.

"How long did you live with your mother?"

"Until I was seventeen," I answered.

"What about your father?" she asked.

"What about him?"

"Did he live with you and your mother?"

"No, he didn't."

"When did you last see him?"

"I never saw him."

"How is that possible?" inquired the psychiatrist.

"I never saw him. I never remember seeing him outside of a photograph I found in a drawer when I was six."

"Do you know why he wasn't around?"

"You'd need to ask Williemaye that question."

Daphne stopped asking questions while she tapped away on her laptop and wrote on a legal pad. She fumbled through a folder and knocked a pile of papers to the floor. She quickly picked them up and tried to put things back in order. After about five minutes of this, Greg made a suggestion. "Let's take a fifteen minute break so Dr. Greene can organize those papers." Daphne agreed, and everyone left the room except her. Fifteen minutes later we were back in the room and Daphne's questions were more to the point.

"Do you feel obligated to your mother?"

"I don't understand what you mean by obligated?" I answered.

"Do you feel like you owe her something, that you are in her debt?" she clarified.

"Hell no!" My anger surprised even me. Greg smiled.

"Do you think she is in your debt, that she owes you?" the psychiatrist inquired.

"She owes me a lifetime of apologies," I countered.

"Why do you think so?"

"She's the town drunk. She embarrassed me every day of my life. Visiting her last Sunday was the worst mistake I ever made in my life. I don't owe her a damn thing."

Ms. Tomkins, Williemaye's lawyer, leaned to her mic. "May I ask a question?"

Greg nodded.

"It needs to be on point," said Daphne.

"I believe it is," said Ms. Tomkins. "Do you believe your mother is crazy?"

"I don't think she's normal by any definition of the word. I studied civil engineering in college. I know how to build roads, bridges, overpasses. If my mother was a bridge, I would ban all traffic until she was torn down and rebuilt."

I held Daphne's gaze for several minutes after my answer. She glanced away, wrote on her legal pad and then looked back at me. "Mr. Oglesby, I'm done. You've been very helpful."

The clock read 8:45 a.m.

Eighteen

Heather and I hugged in the hallway. Greg stood in the corner talking to Mom's attorney. They spoke in whispers that ended with a resounding "No!" from Greg. Mom's lawyer returned to the conference room, and Mom shuffled down the hallway flanked by two large female deputies.

"You two bitches need some deodorant. I've smelled wet hound dogs in heat that smelled sweeter than you two." Mom spoke like she was discussing the weather. Neither of the women seemed to mind, so Mom turned it up a notch. "You know, I bet that your husbands—if someone's been stupid enough to marry either of you—wishes he'd castrated himself after his first night with you."

The taller of the two women made a mistake and countered. "I'll have you know that I've got four grown children and nine grandchildren. No one castrated anybody in our family."

"That explains why they's ugly children in this county. I can't see anything but the ugliest babies coming out of you, and I know your grandkids don't visit zoos 'cause the zookeeper would scoop them up as escapees."

The deputy shook with rage as Mom smiled at her. The other woman took Mom into the conference room. The angry deputy looked at me. "That bitch your mother?"

"I'm sorry to say that she is." She was about to say more to me but Greg waved her off and took Heather and I aside.

"She wants you to testify for Williemaye. And I told her we were not interested," Greg stated.

"Doesn't she know that the judge and Clancy want me to testify against her?"

"I'm pretty sure she simply wants to tangle you up enough so that you do neither," answered Greg. "I also think this isn't the best place to have this conversation," he added.

A guttural "son of a bitch" erupted from the conference room in Mom's distinctive octave. The half-dozen people walking in the hallways stopped as Mom shouted, "Whore bastard! Shit-tongued slut! Ass-snot lip licker!"

I had heard the first two phrases so many times that they sounded trite to me, but to everyone else within earshot, they appeared to have shock value. The last insult of the three was new to me but I wasn't surprised. Mom had a gift. If a contest existed for cursing, Mom would have won against anyone.

The shock wore off, and people walked away. They missed Mom's most creative comments that boomed through the door. "You may be a licensed psychiatrist but your momma spread her legs to the wrong shithead when she made you. You look like someone stuck a wax candle up your ass and made you permanently constipated with your own high opinion of yourself. You need to go get a vibrator and leave it in your butt crack for a week to shake out all the shit you are so full of."

The psychiatrist bolted out of the room as if a fire demon were chasing her. I couldn't see her face but Heather later told me it was streaked with tears. Mom's attorney left next with her briefcase and no expression. Mom stayed inside the room until Deputy Dwayne showed up. He gave me a quick nod as he went into the room. We all waited for another verbal explosion. Nothing happened. Mom walked out of the room with Dwayne on one side and the female deputy on the other. She saw Heather and me holding hands and fumed, "Holding hands in the damn courthouse. Might as well fondle each other in an outhouse."

Heather looked at me, speechless. "That's Mom. "Let's get out of here." I took Heather's hand and we walked out with Greg into the melee of news crews still parked on the courthouse steps.

"We have nothing to say at this time," announced Greg. "But I think Williemaye is going to be allowed to speak to you in a few minutes." The lie bought us enough time to clear the courthouse and move beyond the cameras before the news crews realized they were waiting in vain.

I sat next to Heather in the rental car and watched my hands tremble on the steering wheel. The harder I gripped the steering wheel, the more my hands shook. Heather put her hands on mine, and the shaking stopped after a minute or so. "Let me drive," Heather said softly.

She drove down State Route 85 to Niceville and pulled across the four lanes of John Sims Boulevard into a restaurant parking lot. Heather parked away from the restaurant in a small lot surrounded by live oaks with Spanish moss draping every branch.

The restaurant sat right on the bay, and although the restaurant didn't open for an hour, a server spotted us sitting on the porch. "Y'all like something to drink before we open?" she offered.

"I'd like sweetened ice tea," Heather responded.

"Could I get a couple of beers?" I asked. hopefully

"Y'all musta had a rough morning," said the server with a touch of honest sympathy.

"I had to be in court this morning," I blurted.

The server's face blossomed with recognition. "You're Phil Oglesby! The man they arrested for picking up his mother from church!" She fumbled with her order pad and slipped a blank order form and a pen in front of me. "Could I have your autograph? I've always wanted to meet somebody famous, and here you are at the restaurant where I work!"

I signed and handed her the signature. She looked as if I had handed her a gold coin.

"You don't need to pay for no drinks today. They're on me." She left and returned in one minute with an iced tea for Heather and two chilled bottles of the house brew for me. "I want you to know that my sister and I saw that talk your momma gave in the bar on CNN. It was so plain that she's guilty and that she set you up. I know she's your momma and all, but it's mighty low for any momma to put her son in a spot like that. Mighty low. You've got a lot of people on your side. I'm one of them." She leaned over and hugged Heather. "You must be his wife. You just stand by your man like Tammy Wynette said and it'll all be OK." She patted my shoulder and pranced back inside the restaurant.

I took a long draw on the cold beer, almost burning my throat. It was so cold it should've had chunks of ice in it. The fortified Panhandle Ale didn't freeze because its ethanol content was fifteen percent alcohol. Within a minute, the effects of drinking the bottle in one long, cold gulp hit me.

Some people are nasty drunks like Mom, and some people become maudlin, teary-eyed sentimentalists. I become quiet, and

I don't exactly bubble with the milk of human kindness when I drink. If someone asked me anything at this moment, I'd likely give a fair imitation of Mom. I had enough judgment left to realize that silence and time were my friends while my liver worked to lower my blood alcohol level.

Heather took my chin in her hand and gazed into my eyes before she waved the server over. She handed her the empty second bottle and ordered two coffees. I didn't want to move. And I didn't want lunch. And I didn't want to talk to anyone. Of course, the server told the kitchen crew who was sitting outside. I looked up into a half-dozen friendly faces. The cook reached out to shake my hand. He was a beefy giant who had to weigh over three hundred pounds. "You're eatin' free today. We all think you're a hero." He said the words in the unmistakable accent of a Cajun. "I'm gonna fix y'all the best blackened fish sandwich you ever tasted in your life, and you gotta have my fried bread puddin'."

"You don't have to do that for us," Heather disagreed.

The chef said, "I want to be able to say that I fed the Crestview man who was on CNN. Don't happen every day." I had recovered enough to offer a nod and a "thank you." The chef and his entourage trooped back inside while the server seemed determined to keep us company.

"The most famous person to eat here before you was some TV star from the seventies who retired to Destin before I was even born. Ain't seen none of his old shows but he stops by most Saturdays and some of the tourists ask for autographs, and he is so polite. He just don't like his picture took, that makes him mad. Last time he was here, he had some friends with him and they asked me to photograph them all together and he tipped me a hundred dollars. Biggest tip I ever got. And he don't leave much of a mess like most people."

More customers arrived and by eleven o'clock we were surrounded by tourists and locals watching the sailboats and being pestered by seagulls panhandling at every table. My buzz had passed and when our food arrived I took one bite of the blackened sandwich and blessed the fat chef in the restaurant. Before we finished our sandwiches, the chef brought out the fried bread pudding with Chantilly cream.

"Could I have a picture with y'all to put up on our wall inside?"

Nineteen

Heather drove us back to the hotel, and a divinity must have found something else to occupy the vulture-like news cameras and microphones. Or maybe they were taking a long lunch. The hotel had a modest lobby, and an older woman with silver hair sat in one of two overstuffed chairs. She called my name.

"Phil Oglesby, can I talk to you please?" Her voice had the pronounced twang of a West Florida native, not as honeyed as South Georgia or as nasal as Alabama, but a mixture that sounded like other parts of the South but wasn't. I suspected a local newspaper reporter in disguise. I was wrong.

"What would you like to talk about?" I asked briskly.

"I'd like to talk about you and your mother," she answered.

"I can't think of anything I'd like to talk about less."

"I can understand that but I feel called to talk to you. I really feel called," she replied softly.

I guessed the Almighty himself was in charge of her actions. Some people throw the word *called* around like pennies in an arcade, but this woman didn't seem like that. She looked like she belonged in a Norman Rockwell painting entitled Grandma. Heather intervened.

"We've had a long day, could we talk to you later?"

"I live in old Crestview off Main Street. Can you come over for dinner tonight? Nobody but me and my old cat, Mr. Timmy."

"I don't think it's a good idea for me to discuss my mother with anyone with all the legal problems on my plate," I explained

"I promise to steer clear of your momma's legal troubles and yours. I need to share something else with you," she responded.

"I don't even know your name."

"I've plum forgot all manners. I'm so sorry." She held out her hand. "I'm Oramaye Spence, head of the Women's Auxiliary at Grace Chapel. My granddaddy was the first Pentecostal preacher in this town in 1925."

I shook her hand. "My mom robbed your church," I said softly.

"My son Jack's the head usher. He was in the counting room when your Momma pulled out the pistol," Oramaye said sedately as if she were talking about the weather.

"Mrs. Spence, I think you are probably the last person in the world I should be talking to," I suggested.

"I promise you two things if you come over for supper. One, we won't discuss the robbery, at least not directly, and two, you will taste the best fried chicken in Crestview," she smiled.

"Could you leave us your phone number and address? Phil and I will have to discuss this," answered Heather. Oramaye handed me a slip of paper with an address and a phone number. She gave me a hug and pecked Heather on the cheek.

"Supper's at five thirty. I'm praying that the good Lord will lead you to my table this evening." The automatic doors whooshed behind her.

A few minutes later I dropped face first onto the hotel bed and clutched a pillow as if it were a life vest. I didn't want to talk to Oramaye Spence about Grace Chapel, or her Pentecostal grandfather, or discover why her fried chicken was the best in Crestivew. I wanted to be alone with Heather.

"I don't want to talk to that little old lady," I announced from the bed. Heather sat at the desk in the corner scrolling through emails from her office.

"Call Greg and get his opinion," Heather suggested.

"I don't want to bother him with this," I answered.

"You're going to fret over this the whole afternoon. Greg will probably agree with you. Call him."

Greg's cell rang nine times and he answered just as I was about to press *End*.

"What's on your mind, Phil?"

"A woman named Oramaye Spence surprised us in the hotel lobby. She asked me and Heather to come over for supper."

"I don't think dinner invites fall into the category of legal advice," said Greg with a chuckle.

"I think this one does. She's head of the Women's Auxiliary at Grace Chapel. I got the impression she's up to something. She said she felt called to speak to me."

"I'd say that I don't want you near anyone from that church, but ignoring her might be a bigger mistake than talking to her." The phone went quiet for a minute. I could almost hear Greg thinking about the dilemmas this supper invitation posed. "I don't run in the religious circles around here but most of my best clients do. Let me make some phone calls and find out what I can about Oramaye Spence. I'll get right back to you." Greg clicked off.

I drifted to sleep while Heather plowed through an avalanche of emails from the accounting world. I dreamed I was fourteen and walking along the banks of Live Oak Creek, a pristine cold-water creek that ran for miles before it disappeared into a lime-

125

stone cavern. I sat on the warm sand banks and saw the rarest of animals, an alligator snapping turtle on the opposite bank sunning itself on a log just above the water line. He was enormous, his shell a yard across from front to back. He snoozed in the early afternoon sun while an iridescent dragonfly snatched a moth out of the air and landed on the rugged carapace to eat its prey. The Ice Age denizen opened its lidded eye and stared at me from across the creek. Men had hunted the alligator snappers for generations. Their meat made rich soups and their shells made for bragging rights around fireplaces. This turtle did not fear me. It defiantly slid off the log and hissed as it swam toward me. It wanted me to leave its creek. I stood my ground, and my dream ended before the massive jaws had the chance to bite off half my submerged foot.

Heather shook me awake. "Greg wants to talk to you."

"I think you and Heather should have supper with Oramaye Spence."

"You mind telling me why?" I asked.

"That church is split right down the middle over this robbery. Oramaye is the leader of a faction."

"And I care about that because?"

"Because her group wants to forgive your mother, drop all charges, and make sure that nothing happens to you," Greg offered.

"And what does the other faction want to do?" I queried.

"They want to burn you and Williemaye at a stake in the town square, and something else you ought to know, the pastor of Grace Chapel finagled a meeting with Williemaye this afternoon. Williemaye's lawyer is having fits about it," Greg offered the alert.

"Did the pastor survive the meeting with Mom?"

"I am still trying to find out what happened."

"Out of curiosity, which faction does the pastor belong to?"

"He leads the committee to barbecue you and Williemaye," answered Greg.

Heather made the phone call to Oramaye, promising we'd come to supper that evening. Heather gave me a peck on the cheek and returned to her accounting emails while I fidgeted with the remote control to the TV trying to find something to help me forget why I was still in Crestview. I channel surfed through everything and on my third pass, Heather interrupted.

"I need some quiet to do my work," she said gently. I shut off the TV and went downstairs to find a newspaper or some other distraction. I found neither, so I went back to our room, took the car keys and told Heather that I was headed to the only Starbucks in Crestview, where I bought a large cup of coffee and buried myself in a corner with my cell phone. I had not looked at my emails since Mother's Day and found myself sliding through an avalanche of junk and hellos from people I had known in high school, college, and other slices of the distant past. I lost myself reading until my phone rang.

"We need to be at Oramaye's in fifteen minutes. I'm ready to go," Heather said patiently.

I parked at the curb in front of a shotgun house that saw its prime sixty years earlier, if then. It needed paint, and the enormous live oak shading the home encouraged growth of the large patches of green lichens dotting the worn out shingles on the roof. The flower bed that bordered the porch looked like art, dazzling with red azaleas, blue bonnets, and lilacs. We walked up the cracked concrete sidewalk and knocked on the flimsy door that guarded the screen porch. The front door into the house was open.

"Come on in, it isn't locked," Oramaye rang out cheerfully from inside the home.

We stepped into the front parlor and into another era. Family pictures covered every wall. The clothes and cars in the photos looked like a family history from the 1920s until the early 1960s. The pictures were mute.

"Come on back here in the kitchen," Oramaye called out. We walked on linoleum, older than us, that had a worn pattern resembling a collage of melted candles. Oramaye stood at her stove turning pieces of fried chicken in an iron skillet. She set her Formica dinette table with what I knew must be prized possessions, bone china from an earlier, perhaps more prosperous life, and a cut-glass water pitcher with matching goblets filled with iced tea. She had large buttermilk biscuits on a platter, a jar of open honey, and a triple-layer coconut cake on a pedestal stand. She had gone all out for the man whose mother had robbed her church. She piled the chicken on a platter and supplied our plates with white and dark meat.

"I never ask guests which they prefer since after one bite, they eat all of it," she smiled as she spoke. She took her place at the head of the table and took Heather's hand and mine. She mercifully said the briefest of prayers, and we began eating the best fried chicken I had ever tasted. The biscuits reminded me of a concept from college philosophy, the notion of a perfection that plays out in our world as a dim shadow. Oramaye's biscuits were from that perfect heaven.

After a few minutes she asked why I had decided to come to her home after my earlier reluctance.

"Greg, my lawyer, said you were on my side," I answered.

"Did he now? How'd he find that out?" she asked.

"Greg called clients who knew you," I answered between mouthfuls of potatoes and gravy.

"A lot of people do know me, especially from the church. I supposed you must be wondering why I wanted to meet you."

"I guessed you wanted to talk about my mother and her activities."

"I suppose in a way what I have to say is connected to her and what happened. I asked you here to let you know that I want the church to forgive her and offer her fellowship," Oramaye clarified. A loud knock at the front porch stopped our conversation. Oramaye craned her neck around the corner and frowned. "It's my pastor. Y'all stay right here and I'll be back shortly," she whispered. She hustled to the front porch and opened the door.

"Pastor Williams, I've got company right now," she informed him.

"I am not going to stay long," he bellowed. And then he began a short sermon on the porch. "Williemaye Oglesby belongs in hell. And no church of mine is going to get in her way. She robbed us, she has made a mockery of the law, and she just insulted me this afternoon. I am going to make certain that she goes to jail no matter what you and the members of the Women's Auxiliary think. I am not going to forgive someone who despises me, despises my church, and hates religion. No ma'am, we are not going to forgive Williemaye Oglesby," he announced.

"I don't rightly recall that we are supposed to put conditions on forgiveness," said Oramaye in a clear, piercing voice.

"You didn't hear what she called me when I visited her not less than thirty minutes ago," snarled Pastor Williams.

"And what did she call you?" asked Oramaye without a trace of sympathy.

"I am not going to utter those words in a woman's presence," the pastor replied, with less fire.

"The Good Book says all hidden things will be revealed," countered Oramaye.

"She said I was a fat, puss-gutted son of a bitch! She called me a glutton! She said that I no more belonged in a pulpit than a hemorrhoid did on a Thanksgiving turkey. I offered her salvation and she spewed vulgarity. That woman belongs in hell and we are not going to get in her way!" The pastor's voice slid up several octaves on the last sentence.

"I'm not going to say any more to you today, but if you think you can stay in my church and defend that woman, well you best go find another place to worship!" Pastor Williams dropped the last sentence like it was an anvil. He slammed the screened-in porch door. Heather followed me down the short hallway to Oramaye, who stood on the porch looking at her shattered screen door. It lay across the steps, broken in half. I watched the pastor slam his car door and drive away without a glance at the damage he'd left behind.

"I do believe Pastor Williams is a bit upset," said Oramaye without a hint of anger at herself or the splintered door.

"He tore the door off its hinges," said Heather with some astonishment.

"Men of God do funny things sometimes,"Oramaye shrugged.

I stepped off the porch and set the splintered door to one side. "Do you have any tools?"

"That shed over by the side of the house has got a bushel of tools, but I don't think you're gonna be able to fix that door. It needs a funeral, not a patch," Oramaye exclaimed.

"Mind if I take a look anyway?"

"Suit yourself."

"I haven't been inside that shed for years. Don't really know what's there but you can look," murmured Oramaye.

I had hoped for some nails, a saw, and perhaps some two-by-fours, but in a cobweb-covered back corner I found gold: three replacement screen doors with hinges still attached. I also found hammers, screw drivers, and enough fasteners to make any carpenter grin. In less than an hour I was eating the best coconut cake I had ever tasted while Oramaye admired her new, old screen door.

"Why do you want to forgive Williemaye?" I asked.

"Because we are called to forgive."

"But she robbed your church!"

"I don't rightly see how that makes a difference," answered Oramaye as she sipped ice tea.

"I think it makes a difference in so many ways that I can't count them all."

"It makes no difference to me," answered Oramaye.

"I also think it doesn't matter," I responded.

"Forgiveness always matters. "

"Do you think my Mom wants your forgiveness?"

"She needs it just like you need it." Oramaye replied softly.

"I don't need forgiveness. I didn't rob your church!" I protested.

"I know you didn't rob the church. I'm not talking about forgiving that. I'm talking about you forgiving your mother, that's what really matters here," said Oramaye in slow, measured words.

"Forgive her? She put me in jail," I said with rising heat.

"But you're not in jail anymore," said Oramaye with utter calm.

"The first judge wanted a million dollars in bail and the only reason I'm out now is because I have a good lawyer," I answered firmly.

"The reason you're out may be deeper than a good lawyer. I've been praying for you, and the one message I have for you is simple, forgive your mother."

"Forgive her? Not a chance," I replied with clinched fists.

Twenty

I fell asleep in the hotel bed while Heather worked on her laptop. I woke up every hour to check the clock on the nightstand until sleep finally grabbed me, around three in the morning. Heather woke me after nine o'clock with a cup of hotel-room coffee and a kiss that seemed to say more than good morning, it also said goodbye.

"Corporate needed me back yesterday," Heather said. She began packing her suitcases.

"How long will you be gone?"

"At least a month. They want me to be lead on some accounting headaches," Heather answered.

"With that minister on the warpath, it may be safer in Boston for at least one of us," I grimaced.

"You've got Oramaye and the Women's Auxiliary on your side." Heather pecked me on the cheek.

"After I said no to forgiving Mom, I wouldn't bet any money on how much I can count on Oramaye."

"Oramaye hugged you when we left," answered Heather.

"I think she hugs everyone."

"Maybe she does," Heather closed one suitcase and filled the other. "And maybe she's right about forgiving your mom."

"I wouldn't be in this mess—we wouldn't be in this mess—if you hadn't asked me to forgive her in the first place," I fired without thinking. Heather stiffened like a board.

"This is my fault," she whispered. She finished the last suitcase and headed for the door.

I intercepted her and whispered into her ear, "I'm so damn sorry."

She started crying and shaking, and then I started crying and shaking. Somewhere in the middle of our sobs, we silently forgave each other and knew it without saying a word. It was the oddest moment of my life.

"I still feel like a bug in a spider web," I murmured between kisses.

"Then I'm the bug in the same web next to you," Heather said after another kiss.

We drove to the airport in a deep, warm silence that seemed to feed both of us. She held my right hand while I drove, and I had my right hand on her inner thigh. I ached at the thought of her leaving. We kissed when we got out of the car and kissed again at the security gate. When I got back to the hotel, reality descended. Two news trucks were waiting, and another satellite truck pulled into the parking lot as I opened my car door. I never stood a chance. I had two cameras in my face before I'd walked twenty feet. Several reporters and their crews joined the scrum line before I even understood the questions being thrown at me like volleys by tennis pros.

"Did you know your mother cussed out Grace Chapel's Pastor Williams?" asked a reporter.

"Have you talked to Pastor Williams?" asked another.

"What church do you go to?" asked a new questioner.

"How do you feel about what your mother said to the pastor?" asked the second reporter.

"I don't know Pastor Williams, and I had no idea that he was going to talk to Williemaye. I am sorry if she insulted him." I hoped my answer would end the inquisition. It didn't.

"Have you talked to Pastor Williams?" fired an insistent reporter.

"No, and I think I would need to talk to my lawyer before I had any conversation like that," I answered.

"Do you go to church?" repeated the same reporter.

"I haven't been in years," I answered.

"Then you had never been to Grace Chapel before Mother's Day?"

"I've never been inside Grace Chapel," I corrected.

"Why do you think your mother robbed Grace Chapel?" asked another reporter.

"I can't answer that question."

A blur of questions followed, all focused on the robbery, Mom's anger at the pastor, and churches in general. I raised my hand and made a final statement. "I can't answer any more questions. I wish none of this had ever happened." I ignored the cameras, microphones, and reporters, and jogged into the hotel.

The assistant manager at the front desk caught my eye as I walked through the micro lobby. She waved me over and startled me with a question.

"When do you plan on leavin'?" she asked.

"That depends on this little legal problem I have. Why do you need to know?"

"Corporate called not five minutes ago. They wanted to know when you was leaving. I was watching you on TV while those reporters was asking you all them questions. The phone rang about you and it was my boss's boss's boss asking how long you planned to stay," she explained.

"Why do they care about when I leave?"

"I asked the same question. They said you riled up some people 'round here and it might be bad for business to have you stayin' here much longer. I told them you was quiet and didn't cause no trouble, but that didn't seem to count for much."

"They don't want me staying here because I've upset someone?"

"That's the problem," she agreed.

"When do I have to leave?" I asked, bewildered.

"Your wife paid the account through next Thursday so you're good until then," she answered.

"You mean I can't stay beyond that?"

"I don't think so. They didn't tell me exactly that you couldn't stay but they said somethin' about needin' to renovate that part of the hotel where you're stayin'. To my mind, they're interested in gettin' you to leave. I'm sorry about that 'cause despite what I've heard some people say, you seem like a good guy," she sympathized.

"What have you heard some people say?"

"You sure you want to hear this?" she asked solemnly.

I nodded.

"I've heard people say you're a communist, a socialist, a member of a terrorist group. Bunches of people said you must be an atheist and that you put your momma up to the robbery as some kind of publicity stunt for somebody." She said this in a low, conspiratorial voice.

"None of that is true," I denied softly. "I came here because my wife asked me to see my mom."

"Hard to believe somethin' as simple like that could cause so much trouble."

"Yes, it is. I'll find somewhere else to stay." I muttered without anger and went to my room.

My stomach tightened into a knot. I was about to be kicked out of a hotel. Considering my luck, it was overdue. I was just a guy with a jail record for picking up his mother from church. The situation fit together like a jigsaw puzzle of a car wreck. I sighed.

I sauntered to my room and fell onto the bed. It was early afternoon and thunderheads were building on the horizon outside my window. Heather leaving, the press ambush, and losing the room hit me. I lay on the bed and closed my eyes. Booming thunder woke me. I glanced at the clock. I had slept for hours. Lightning slashed across the sky and exploded a palm tree just outside my window. The shockwave shook the window, and the thunder hit me in the chest like an anvil. Dazed, I watched the storm rage. The shattered stump of the palm tree smoldered as rain sheeted against my window. My stomach growled. I had skipped breakfast and lunch. I hoped the restaurant across the parking lot had not adopted an anti-Phil policy too.

Inside the restaurant the hostess gave me a spot in a corner away from the supper crowd of families. I sensed stares as I followed her to my table. Someone whispered, "He's the one with his momma in jail." Before the server finished my order, I had seen at least five cell phone flashes aimed at me. My first urge was to do a Williemaye and call them all assholes. But I wasn't Mom. She would've emptied the restaurant with her volcanic tongue. I'd only insult people and have some local pound me into the pavement for my trouble. When the server brought my sweetened ice tea and smothered steak, dozens of eyes were watching me.

I stood up and made a speech to the throng. "I don't know y'all but y'all seem to be interested in me. I'm Phil Oglesby, born here in Crestview. I visited my mother on Mother's Day and it's caused me a lot of trouble. I would like to eat without being stared at or having flashes go off in my face. I hope y'all will let me eat my supper in peace."

An awkward quiet spread around me until the silence had a texture like a blanket. When I raised my head, the eyes were focused on their plates and families. I ate alone and unwatched. My cell phone rang as I paid my check.

"Phil, can you drop by my office in a few minutes? I need to run some developments by you," Greg informed me.

"What kind of developments?"

"Don't know if it's good news or bad. Well, probably good," Greg pondered.

"You can't give me a hint?"

"If we can get all parties to agree, you may not have to live here for six months pending the trial," answered Greg.

"Six months!" The cashier handed me my receipt and I scooted outside.

"You said this might be over in a week or two! What's happened?"

"That's what we need to talk about," Greg revealed.

"I'll be there in a few minutes unless lighting strikes me, which I hope it does."

"Be careful with that idea because most people think you been hit already," Greg suggested.

Twenty-One

I parked in front of the office. Two ancient magnolias guarded the sidewalk that led to his front door. Greg owned the corner building on the block in the heart of the oldest part of Crestview, and his building stood out for its 1920s red-brick façade with old paneled double front doors that might have been more at home on an antebellum mansion in the country. The storm had left the air humid, like moist layers of steamy curtains. I reached the front doors dripping with sweat, rang a buzzer, and Greg welcomed me into his air-conditioned haven.

He offered me a seat on the sofa instead of the chair in front of his desk. He poured us a cup of coffee and added a dash of whiskey to his.

"Would you like a shot?"

"I'll get by with the caffeine, but I bet Mom would love to have the opportunity," I smirked.

"That brings up a small mystery. I think everyone knows Williemaye is a professional alcoholic, world class, and she's been in jail long enough to have some serious withdrawals, perhaps worse," mused Greg. " I'm sure they'd take her to the hospital," I answered.

"I'd have heard if that'd happened. I suspect something else is going on," replied Greg.

"What could that be?"

"That goes to the point of why we need to talk. I think the jail might be doing some preventive medication to keep her under control," answered Greg.

"You mean they're giving her bourbon?"

"That's my guess, and the reason's simple: They don't expect to have to deal with her much longer," explained Greg.

"Has she agreed to a plea bargain?" I asked incredulously. Williemaye loved attention, and for the first time in her life, she was the center of it. I couldn't see her agreeing to be reasonable.

"It's almost like that but it isn't. Grace Chapel doesn't like this publicity, Tallahassee doesn't like it, and nobody that matters in Crestview likes it with the exception of Williemaye," said Greg, smiling. He went to his desk and brought back a letter, handed it to me, and poured some whiskey into my coffee.

"Read that and tell me what you think."

District Attorney Clancy had sent the letter to Greg. Clancy recommended all parties agreed to an expedited trial with Judge Hightower and no jury. Given the community interest in resolving this problem, Clancy was willing to drop all charges against me in return for my willingness to testify for the state. He also mentioned that charges against Williemaye would not be as inclusive as he first intended. Ms. Tompkins had already agreed to accommodate the expedited trial process, and only a few witnesses would be called, including an usher from the church, Deputy Dwayne, the clerk from Mossy Head General Store, and me. The trial date was Friday, two days away.

"I'll be dipped in pig shit," I murmured.

"That beats being tarred and feathered," Greg suggested.

141

"I don't like the idea of testifying against Mom, but it sounds like this may be the only way I can get out of Crestview," I said in a hushed voice.

"That was my recommendation as your friend and lawyer."

"Solves another problem for me. I'm about to be kicked out of my hotel. I'll only need someplace to stay for as long as the trial lasts. Am I right that they want this over in two or three days?"

"It could be faster than that, Hightower may already know what he intends to do,"Greg proposed.

"And then I can leave?"

"And then you can leave," Greg confirmed.

"Any suggestions about where I can stay until then?"

"That's another small miracle. I have a house available and it's unoccupied."

"I didn't know you were a landlord," I probed.

"I'm not. It's Williemaye's, and it still isn't foreclosed on. You might as well stay there for free."

We drove in separate cars to Mom's home on Third Street. Every home on the street had neatly clipped yards with flower beds, trimmed shrubs, and live oaks older than Methuselah. Porch lights glowed in front of every home except Williemaye's. Overgrown weeds, grass a yard high, and darkness cloaked Williemaye's home like a blanket. I parked on the cracked concrete driveway, and Phil met me at the front door.

"I know it looks like hell, but it's mostly clean inside. I managed to get Gulf Power to turn on the lights this morning," Greg stated as he unlocked the front door.

"Where'd you get the keys?" We entered the parlor that held countless bad memories for me.

"Deputy Dwayne got 'em for me. He is a good man, and I think he's on our side."

"Counting you and Lynette, that makes three," I said without humor.

"You're forgetting Oramaye Spence."

"OK, four then. I thought this hellhole was supposed to be foreclosed." I opened the refrigerator and found it full of Tupperware filled with meals and two six-packs of beer.

"Bank of West Florida and their attorneys are a little reluctant to do that until the dust settles on this case. Also, Williemaye's little ATM deposit caused some processing problems for reasons that their counsel is reluctant to discuss. Ms. Tompkins knows more than she is telling, but I have half a notion that Williemaye might get this place back after she serves her time."

"Who do I owe for the food?" I asked.

"That's from Lunette and one of her girlfriends. You are going to eat better than anyone else in Crestview for the next few days."

I offered Greg a beer but he begged off and left me with a promise to come by the following evening to discuss my testimony. He gave me the keys and left me alone in the home I had always hated.

I drove back to the hotel, cleaned out my room, and gleefully checked out. It was nearly midnight by the time I locked the front door to Williemaye's home and set my suitcase down in the bedroom I had left twenty-two years earlier. Exhaustion made me collapse on a spongy, old mattress covered with a quilt that moths had almost devoured. But I couldn't sleep.

I stayed awake for an hour reliving my last night in the house, twenty-two years earlier when I left for college in another state away from Crestview, away from Mom. Mom had been sitting in the kitchen with a half-bottle of whiskey. She drank without a glass, chugging the amber fluid in huge gulps. I had ignored her on the way to my room, closed the door, pulled out an old trunk I'd found for a few dollars at a thrift store, and began to pack every scrap of clothes I owned. I saved my new suit for last. I had worked two jobs that summer and saved enough to buy the suit at Sears. Through the closed bedroom door, I had heard Mom drinking and muttering curses to herself. Sometime after ten o'clock, she bellowed, "Where's the damn bottle?" She opened and slammed every cabinet door in the kitchen, and a brief silence descended when she found a fresh pine to suck dry. Between gulps, she fired off several salvos for my benefit.

"The little, sniveling, ungrateful, snot-sucking bastard I carried in my belly is leaving me. The bastard that tore me open so bad they had to stitch me up, the bastard who used to suck at my tits for his dinner is leaving me. That's what I get for being a mother."

Her words had sliced the air like daggers but I had heard it all so many times I ignored her. I packed. Williemaye muttered some more in the kitchen, shattered an empty bottle against a wall, and then went silent. I knew that bourbon and exhaustion had finally won out. She had not been awake the next morning when I left before dawn for the bus station.

I slept in Momma's vacant house until sunlight warmed my face the next morning. A mockingbird was running through its repertoire of sounds, from a car alarm to a seagull's cry. I turned over when I heard a knock on the door. It repeated four or five times before I dragged my rumpled soul to the door and made the mistake of opening the door without glancing out a side window first. A reporter I recognized from the hotel parking lot greeted me with her camera crew; another guy from another station was jostling to get beside her. I closed the door in their faces, heard thumps, curses, more thumps, and a couple of thuds while I searched the kitchen for some coffee.

Williemaye had an open can of ground coffee that smelled like aged cat piss on the counter. I wanted coffee but not with that aroma. I searched and found an unopened jar of freeze-dried decaffeinated coffee that probably dated back to Clinton's presidency. I tried to tease some crystals out but they formed a solid brown mass in the jar. I boiled water and poured some in the jar, teasing out enough coffee syrup to make a cup of java that tasted surprisingly good. I had gulped half of it when I heard the tap at the kitchen window. I ignored the tap until I heard Deputy Dwayne's distinctive twang.

"Phil, I got better things to do than stand out here and bang on your window all morning."

I pulled back the dust-laden curtains and waved Dwayne to the back door. I opened the door expecting to see news crews trailing Dwayne, but he was alone.

"How'd you avoid the vultures in the front yard?" I asked.

"I saw the fight on your doorstep and pulled them aside for a little discussion about disorderly conduct, trespassing, assault, and disturbing the peace. I told those crazy sonsabitches to stay off this property. So they all gathered themselves up and planted themselves along the sidewalk. Three new trucks drove up when the first batch got back to the curb. Gave them the same speech. One of them's calling some lawyer they use. Told them they could call anyone they wanted as long as they stay off your porch."

"How'd you know to rescue me?"

"Didn't rightly know you needed rescuin' but the sheriff sent me by to let you know that Clancy would like to talk to you," Dwayne responded.

"I don't think that's a good idea," I answered.

"I have some ideas on that subject but first, could I have a cup of coffee?"

I warned Dwayne about the coffee but after a sip, he told me that it was better than what he usually had to drink at the sheriff's office.

"Why does Clancy want to talk to me, and why is the sheriff sending you to let me know?"

"I told Robbie he oughta go through your lawyer. He pitched a fit like a two-year-old with fire ants on his pecker. Said I worked for him, not some attorney with less brains than a dog turd. I don't think I'm going to support him next time he runs for office," Dwayne stated.

"Why does he care whether or not I talk to Clancy?"

"They back scratch each other all the time," Dwayne said with a broad grin.

"When does Clancy want to see me?"

"This afternoon, about two o'clock in his office. It's right next to the courthouse. But I suspect you know not to show up without Greg, and if Greg can't make it on such short notice, I'd advise you to have him tell Clancy to forget it," Dwayne counseled.

I looked at Deputy Dwayne and realized I had another friend that I had not expected to find.

"What about that crowd out in front of the house?"

"Tell you what we're gonna do. You check with Greg, slip out this back door, walk straight through your back yard, and meet me in front of the street that's behind you," Dwayne offered.

"You going to chauffer me around all day?"

"It'll keep me away from the office and you away from the press. We both win," Dwayne chuckled.

He waited while I called Greg, who was not happy with Clancy's tactic.

"I'll call him and explain that even though you're a witness for the prosecution, I'm still your attorney and he has to go through me. And we are not seeing him until courts in session. He's going to have to live with that. He can fax me the questions and you and I can rehearse your answers this evening," Greg said without taking a breath.

"Isn't this likely to make him mad?" I worried.

"He's always mad. I don't trust him with any client of mine sitting in his office answering questions. He can wait to ask the questions he wants to in front of the judge with me present," Greg answered. He also told me to drop by his office after four o'clock that afternoon for some advice on my testimony.

"Greg said I'm not seeing Clancy today,"

Dwayne nodded and exited by the front door. The crowd in front shouted questions as Dwayne gave a short news conference. He was buying me time to escape unnoticed. I slipped out the back door, walked around a clothesline draped with sheets and towels, startled a beagle sleeping under the porch, and ran to the street in front of the home with the dog at my heels, announcing my presence to all the world. No one paid attention. No one opened a door or window along either side of the street. A barking dog in daylight didn't have much value in this neighborhood. Dwayne's police cruiser turned the corner down the street, and he drove at a slow pace. He knew a speeding deputy would draw attention. He picked me up without fanfare.

Twenty-Two

Dwayne drove to Jimmy's Waffles and Eggs on the northern edge of town. "Best breakfast in Crestview, and nobody pays attention to nobody unless you start the conversation. "

Regulars filled every table so we took stools at the counter where the short-order cook gave Dwayne a look, wrote an order on his pad, and raised an eyebrow at me.

"Danny wants to know what you want to eat?" asked Dwayne

"Eggs, sausage, and grits."

The cook nodded and went to work. Dwayne poured us cups of coffee from the carafe on the counter and got the stink eye from a server at the far end.

"Dwayne just 'cause you're a lawman don't give you the right to steal coffee," she complained, in mock offense.

"It's a compliment to you, Beulah Belle, because you have the only coffee worth stealing in all of Crestview," answered Dwayne.

Beulah brought over a bottle of hot sauce and chili flakes for Dwayne, who baptized his eggs and sausage with both when she set his plate in front of him.

"Why do you ruin good food with all that pepper?" she asked.

"I like my food extra spicy, just like my women," answered Dwayne.

"If your wife, Dora, hears you say that, I think your spicy days will come to a mighty quick end," Beulah fired back.

"Dora don't mind what I say as long as I leave it at the sayin'," smiled Dwayne.

Beulah left to clean tables and take a new raft of orders as more customers in work clothes filled every open seat.

"Would you like to know how your momma's doing in jail?" asked Dwayne.

"Not especially." I took a bite of the best country sausage I had ever eaten.

"I can understand that but she sure has made life interesting while she's been there," Dwayne snickered.

"Not sure I enjoy her idea of interesting," I replied.

"We had some problems at first. She made lots of people cry, especially the female staff. Denise Twerfer, our head matron, tried to be nice one day by showing pictures of her grandkids to Williemaye.

Williemaye took one look at the pictures and told Denise that she had the ugliest grandkids in the county, wanted to know what made her think Williemaye wanted to see something as pathetic looking as them kids, and asked her why they was not wearing bags over their ugly little heads when they was in public. Denise cried and asked Williemaye why she was being so mean. Williemaye said she was the mean one showing Williemaye those ugly kids before lunch. Said she couldn't eat now after seeing them ugly kids. We had to send Denise home for the rest of the day. Williemaye and I had a talk after that. I asked her what it would take to get her to settle down. I warned her that this was a Southern jail, and some of the people who worked in it might decide to work her over if she kept this up. Williemaye told me

Mother's Day

that if she got a scratch or a bruise, she'd make sure it was on CNN before sundown."

"That sounds like Mom."

"I did find something that mostly works," Dwayne continued.

"Bourbon?"

"Greg musta told you," answered Dwayne.

"You negotiated the Crestview Jailhouse Bourbon Peace Treaty with Williemaye Oglesby?"

"A fifth a day and she promised not to hurt anyone's feelin's, at least not intentionally."

"Who's paying for the bourbon?"

"We have more seized dope money than we know what to do with," Dwayne answered. "Had one sheriff that could not help himself shortly after you left town in the late eighties. He bought hisself a cabin cruiser down in Destin with one pile of that seized money. He'd of gotten away with it if he hadn't been cheatin' on his wife with some waitress he met in Niceville. The wife blew the whistle and things got right nasty real fast. Sheriff ended up losing his job, the boat, and his wife," Dwayne informed me wistfully.

"So Momma robbed a church to end up in jail drinking bourbon paid for by dope money seized by the sheriff's office?"

"That is one way to look at it. It is amazing what's happened since she pulled that pistol in Grace Chapel," agreed Dwayne. "People knew about Destin, Pensacola, and Fort Walton before this happened, but now, thanks to Williemaye, people know about Crestview," added Dwayne.

"People should know to stay the hell away," I said firmly.

"You have a right to be sore about this, more than a right. But if life is about living and excitement, you have been to on one hell of a carnival ride since you came to town."

"I don't see a million-dollar bail and nights in jail as a carnival ride," I answered.

"Carnival ain't quite the right word, but so many people are so damned bored, so tired of life, so angry at themselves, that they wishes they was dead, or they go beyond wishin' and make themselves dead," Dwayne commented.

"I don't see your point," I answered.

"My point is that Williemaye did something that gave you a level of excitement, a dose of aggravation that turned you on like a spotlight. When we were talking at the curb outside the church your eyes were dead. You looked like a man that life had grabbed by the throat and just about choked to death. Williemaye dragging you into that robbery was wrong, bad wrong, but it gave you a jolt that changed you. I saw it in the squad car after that stand-off at the Mossy Head General Store. It made you look a lot more interested in living than when I first saw you that Sunday morning."

"I wasn't suicidal. I hadn't worked in six months, and I need-ed a job. I still need one. I didn't need three nights in jail," I replied.

"All I know is that I saw a man who was lower than a corpse in a deep hole," Dwayne remarked. He sipped his coffee and refilled my cup. "And now you're famous," he added with a grin.

"Famous for driving the getaway car for Mom after she robbed a church," I shot back.

"I know you are innocent, and I think this is gonna work out OK for you. It's only a feelin' but I believe it's true. You're gonna be fine when all this is over," he insisted.

We finished breakfast and strolled back to the patrol car.

"You want to ride along with me today? I could use the company and I'm a guessin' that you could use the distraction," Dwayne offered.

"You sure you want to be seen with me?"

"I can always say that I was keepin' you under close surveillance," answered Dwayne.

I almost said, "Are you?" but some shred of judgment held the question on the tip of my tongue. Southern lawmen are usually depicted as idiotic or corrupt, and Crestview had seen more than its share of both. But Dwayne was no idiot, and no one had enough money to corrupt him. I realized that a day spent with him was a day spent with someone I could trust.

"I am in your debt," was my answer.

Twenty-Three

"Why are we headed to Mossy Head?" I asked as we cruised down State Route 85.

"I figure it can't hurt to give you a chance to look at that place one more time before you have to testify."

"I remember what happened. I fell asleep in the car while Williemaye went inside. I woke up, walked into the store, saw the cashier at the counter watching TV and eating fried pie while drinking a soda. And there was Mom, shoving cash into the damn ATM. I went over and found checks that Mom had tossed to the floor, all of them made out to Grace Chapel.

Shortly after that I saw the news bulletin on the TV and motioned the clerk over, who went white faced when I pointed to the TV," I said slowly.

"I still want you to see the place, and I think you oughta ask that cashier what happened to the money in the ATM," Dwayne suggested.

"Why do I care about the money?"

"It's just amusing, considering everything else that has happened," Dwayne noted.

"And you don't want to tell me?"

"I want you to hear it from the cashier," answered Dwayne.

Dwayne had to park on the other side of the road from the Mossy Head General Store. Cars, buses, RVs, and pickups jammed the front, sides, and back of the store. Inside three cashiers were selling photos of the store with a man standing in front of the store holding a dead opossum. I learned a few minutes later that it was the rabid opossum that Mom had shot. The spot where Mom had killed the opossum had a small dais where tourists were jostling one another in a line to have their picture taken with a stuffed opossum that wore a name tag: Williemaye's pet. Picnic tables surrounded a large barbecue grill out back, and two men barbecued while several servers took orders and served customers. A man at the closest cash register caught my eye and waved me and Dwayne over.

"I am so glad to see you," the man said as he offered his hand.

"I'm Darryl LaRue, and you have done so much for my business. I've had to hire help, bring in the barbecue crew, and extend my hours. You and your momma put this place on the map. I'm grateful. You and Dwayne got to have some barbecue on me before you leave," he said cheerfully before returning to the long line at his register.

Dwayne looked around and spotted the cashier he wanted me to see. She was restocking the beer case, which was nearly empty.

"Darryl, you mind if we talk to Emma Jo for a few minutes?" Dwayne asked the harried man.

"You're completely welcome to but could you help her put in the beer?" answered Darryl.

Dwayne nodded, and we wordlessly joined Emma Jo and filled the glass-front beer cooler together. When we finished, Emma Jo invited us to sit at a small table in the back of the store where she poured both of us quart-sized cups of sweetened ice tea.

"I asked Deputy Dwayne to bring you out here for two reasons," Emma Jo smiled. "I'm famous now. I've had people askin' for my picture and my autograph, and Darryl is so happy that he's made me assistant manager and gave me a raise," she added.

"I'm glad you've been lucky but what did you need to tell me?" I asked.

"All this happened because you drove your momma here, she shot that possum, and all those news trucks showed it on TV. Darryl hasn't got any money for advertising so he was close to layin' me off. I need this job. I go to Northwest Florida College, and this pays for my books and gas," she explained.

"Emma Jo, I'm glad you kept your job and can stay in school, but you said you had two reasons to talk to me. What's the other one?" I asked.

"Nobody knows how much money your momma put in that ATM," she said in a hushed voice.

"I don't understand . . . that doesn't make any sense," I answered.

Dwayne put his hand on my shoulder. "Let her explain, it gets better."

"I heard about this from my aunt who works at the bank as a loan officer. The day after you and your Momma was arrested, the bank sent an armored truck out here to take the ATM and give us a replacement. They took that ATM to the bank and rolled it into a back room, pried it open and began to count the cash. The machine was filled and it had jammed. The ATM has a satellite connection to a secure database which is in Mumbai, India. The ATM is supposed to keep a record of all the cash it gives out and all the deposits it takes in. The company in India that has the satellite link had a main server crash just as your momma began her deposit. Somebody in Eastern Europe, they think it was the Ukraine, hacked into their network and created an electronic hurricane. Codes were lost, passwords stolen, and systems crashed. They got no records for any of the transactions on that ATM for that day. Nothing at all."

"Doesn't the bank have some record of what happened?" I asked.

"No, and they don't want people to know about it," she whispered.

"So what happened to all the money she deposited into the ATM?"

"Nobody at the bank knows what money belongs to Grace Chapel and what money belongs to the bank," she answered. "They got some computer whizzes from Florida State that came in to help and there's a man from India staying in town trying to sort it out, but I don't think they are ever going to really know exactly how much was there," she answered.

"Can't they just count the money in the ATM and work back from that, at least make an educated guess?"

"That might have worked if they'd been a little quicker and a little more careful," Emma Jo added with a smile.

"What do you mean by quicker and more careful?"

"Once they saw the jammed money, they gave up for the day and stopped trying to count. They stored the ATM in a part of the bank that didn't have a sprinkler system. A circuit in the wall shorted out, caught the machine on fire—caught the whole ceilin' on fire—and pretty much burned up most of the money in that

ATM before the fire department got there to put it out," she said with a smile.

Dwayne and I ate barbecue ribs, and I had my picture taken with Darryl, Emma Jo, and the stuffed opossum. On the drive back from Mossy Head, my head was spinning as I thought about all that had happened. I asked Dwayne what he thought about the ATM, the computers crashing, and the fire that burned up all the money.

"I think it was an act of God," Dwayne replied without a trace of a smile.

Twenty-Four

I asked Dwayne to drop me off at the house so I could pick up the car. He glanced at his watch. It was almost two o'clock.

"I bet I can drop you off in front," he offered.

"You think they've given up by now?"

"Florida sun, daytime mosquitoes, and biting flies? That reporter crowd ain't made like the old timers. They've all gone for a long lunch, but don't be a bit surprised if they don't come knockin' at your door this evening or try again early tomorrow morning," Dwayne warned.

No satellite trucks were in sight when Dwayne turned the corner to Clifford Drive. He let me out in Mom's overgrown driveway.

"Thanks for rescuing me this morning."

"You rescued me. Robbie wanted me to go over to that damn bank today and take pictures of that burned ATM machine. I understand the room stinks something terrible. They used foam to put out that fire that smells like a cross between cat piss and vomit. And it ain't been cleaned up yet, so I told Robbie that I needed to check on you and needed to check on a disturbance complaint in Mossy Head. It worked out best for the both of us," Dwayne said with a wink and a smile, and then he drove off.

The news crews had left a dozen business cards taped to the front door and the front windshield of my rental car. Those bastards were not giving up. I scooped all the cards up and tossed them in a weed-filled flower pot at the side of the house. I opened the front door, and someone tapped me on the shoulder. I spun around expecting to have a microphone and a camera stuck in my face. Instead, I saw an old woman wearing an ankle length skirt, long sleeves, a sun bonnet, and a mostly toothless smile.

"Didn't mean to scare you, Phil Oglesby. Don't you remember me? I'm Eulah Raye Clemens. I live across the street."

I remembered her. Mom hated everyone on the street, and they hated her back. And to stay out of Mom's way, everyone mostly ignored me. Except Eulah Raye. She gave me a coat one winter when she saw me walking to school wearing just a shirt and an old pair of jeans. She never tangled with Mom but whenever she saw me, she waved and smiled. I never knew much about her or her life, though.

"You gave me a coat one winter."

"I do seem to recall that I didn't have any use for it. Would you like to come over to my kitchen for some pecan pie and ice cream?" she asked.

I followed Eulah Raye across the street to a yard that contrasted Mom's. Rows of flowers bordered the sidewalk to the front door, shrubs were trimmed to perfection in squares and rectangles, and there were no weeds. The throw rugs on the ancient yellow pine floors looked older than Methuselah, and her kitchen linoleum had worn through in spots, revealing an ancient subfloor stained black. She cut a huge slice of pecan pie for me and buried it under four scoops of vanilla ice cream. She cut a piece for herself and poured us ice tea. She didn't say a word until I took a bite of the pie with the ice cream. It tasted like heaven.

"I was hopin' to get to talk to you. I seen what happened to you on TV at that first hearing. I called Oramaye Spence right then and told her I watched you grow up and there was no way you would ever rob no church. No way at all. That hearin' was the most ridiculous thing I ever seen in my life, puttin' you in jail and lettin' Williemaye walk out scot-free just to go to a bar and drink herself silly while her son sits in jail because he picked her up from church. I am so sorry that you had to go through that," Eulah Raye told me between sips of tea. She inhaled her pie and was downing a second slice while I had only plowed through half of mine.

"I thought most people around here figured that I must be guilty," I answered with a mouthful of pie.

"Mostly they're ignorant. They figure Williemaye's crazy and that her son can't be much different. I never seen you that way. Seen you go to school every day. Take any job you could find while you were in high school. And I seen you leave that morning for college. I hoped you'd never have to come back. Not to a home like that one across the street," Eulah Raye spoke softly.

"I stayed away as much as I could. I spent summers working on construction jobs. Became a land surveyor. Once I had my degree, I went north to be a civil engineer. I felt guilty about not coming around to check on Mom, but, I didn't see the point in visiting. It would have been better if I had stuck to that," I commented.

"She didn't improve after you left, that's for certain. Williemaye scared all the Mormon missionaries away from the street, and even the Jehovah's Witnesses gave up on her and the whole block," exclaimed Eulah Raye.

"How'd she do that?" I asked.

"I don't rightly know about the Mormons and what she said to them, but I was in the front yard weedin' my flower bed when a Jehovah's Witness couple knocked on your momma's door about ten in the morning. Williemaye told them to shove their magazine and their books up their butts with a baseball bat dipped in flaming dog shit. I am sorry to use that word but you could hear Williemaye cuss them poor folks for a hundred yards in all directions. I don't care much for them witnesses, but they didn't deserve the beatin' she gave them. They stood frozen there at her door while she ranted like that for five minutes. She slammed the door in their faces when she was done, and they stood there shaking. They walked real slow to their car and drove off. The woman was cryin' and the man had a look on his face I really can't describe," commented Eulah Raye.

"That sounds like my mom."

"But you ain't like that. I never heard you cuss growing up, and no one ever talked about you drinkin' or carryin' on like someone who'd lost their mind."

"I nearly lost my mind on this trip," I answered.

"I been prayin' for you and so has most of the Women's Auxiliary. I believe it's gonna come out alright for you. I really do."

I stayed until I had to go to Greg's office. I showed Eulah Raye pictures of Heather, our townhouse in Boston, and our dog, Slippers. She showed me pictures of her family. Eulah was a great-grandmother with four living children, all successful and living far away. She showed me pictures of the last Thanksgiving at her house and the crowd that filled every corner at Christmas.

She told me that her kids wanted her to move to be closer to at least one of them but she didn't want to leave her church or her memories. She gave me a peck on the cheek when I left and told me to bring Heather by to see her the next time that Heather was in town.

Greg's secretary greeted me at the door and walked me to his office. He was tapping away at his computer screen and drinking coffee. He nodded and pointed to a chair next to his desk. I waited while he finished up whatever he was doing on his computer. I looked at a nearby wall covered with family pictures from vacations, birthdays, and college days. The picture in the very center of the collection was from high school. Greg and I were at graduation, each holding our diplomas, and he had his arm draped around his younger brother, Michael, who killed himself a few years later. Michael was a loner, a gifted student who went to Florida State, dropped out, disappeared, and killed himself in a shabby hotel in Dothan, Alabama. Greg and I never talked about it, but it changed Greg in ways I hadn't expected, one being he left the church he had spent his life attending.

Greg closed his laptop, retrieved a legal pad from the pile on the floor, and told his secretary to lock up and go home for the day.

"I don't know that this matters but I learned some things to-day that you probably ought to know," I offered.

"Shoot."

"The ATM at the Mossy Head General Store, the one Williemaye stuffed with the cash she robbed from Grace Chapel, burned up in a fire in some back room of a bank. They did not get the money out first."

"It's like that money had a curse on it," Greg commented with a wry smile.

"There's more. Someone in Eastern Europe hacked the offshore data managing system in India, causing a crash that pretty much obliterated transactions for the bank on that Sunday at that ATM," I added.

"Those systems have backups for the backups. There is going to be a record somewhere," he added.

"That doesn't appear to be the case," I replied.

"You mind telling me who told you this stuff?" asked Greg.

"Cashier at the store in Mossy Head. Her aunt works at the bank. She asked me not to involve her for obvious reasons but she wanted me to know," I answered.

"This story gets better every day. Grace Chapel wants this over quick because they don't want any questions that could lead to questions about their bookkeeping, finances, or accountability. The state judiciary wants it over because the first hearing made Florida judges look like contestants on the Gong Show, and now the bank has a little problem it doesn't want discussed on the evening news," Greg said with a smile cracking his face.

His smile led to a laugh, and the laughter produced tears. It was contagious. I began laughing until I was rolling on the plush carpet and my sides were hurting. Ten minutes later we were gasping for breath and coming back to earth. Then Greg got serious.

"If I was Williemaye's lawyer, I would drive all these people crazy with questions they would never want to answer. I would delay this thing until they begged for a plea bargain that released Williemaye for time served in the local jail," he proposed. "And I might ask them to return the money all the deputies snatched out of the air and off the pine trees at the Mossy Head General Store parking lot," he added.

"How much did they collect from that bag Robbie had me dump out?" I asked.

"A tad under three hundred thousand dollars. All in hundreds and fifties. And that's a number not for distribution at the present time," Greg responded.

"You add that to Williemaye's deposit and you have quite an offering," I added.

"Williemaye did make a dent, that's for sure, but I still need to prep you for this trial, if that is what it should be called. I jotted down these questions from a phone call with Clancy, and he promised he'd stick to this list. Let's start. Did you pick up Williemaye Oglesby from Grace Chapel on Mother's Day? You are going to say yes. Did Williemaye have anything with her? Your answer is another yes. What did she have with her?" asked Greg, motioning for me to answer.

"She had a zippered shopping bag," I answered.

"Did you know what was in it?"

"No, I didn't."

"Where did you go after Grace Chapel," asked Greg.

"The Mossy Head General Store."

"Why did you go there?" asked Greg.

"Mom asked me to take her there."

"Didn't you think that was an odd request?"

"Yes I did, but Mom put up a fuss and I drove to Mossy Head to keep the peace," I answered.

"What happened when you reached Mossy Head?"

"Mom had me stop at the general store, and I fell asleep in the car."

"What happened when you woke up?"

"I went inside the store," I answered.

"What did you see inside the store?"

"I saw Mom taking money out of the shopping bag and tossing checks on the floor."

"What was Williemaye doing with the money?"

"She was feeding the bills into the ATM."

"Where did she get the money?"

"I didn't know until I looked at one of the checks on the floor. The first one I picked up was made out to Grace Chapel for one thousand dollars. I asked Mom what the hell was going on.

She admitted that she'd taken the money from the church. Then I looked at the TV set above the cash register and saw a news flash announcing the robbery of Grace Chapel. They flashed a picture of Mom from the security system inside the church. That's when I knew she had robbed the church," I said.

"That's all of it. Clancy ought to be satisfied with that." Greg established.

"What's going to happen to Mom?" I asked.

"There's a deal on the table. If she were to plead guilty before the trial, I doubt she'd get more than a few years," answered Greg.

"What if she doesn't plead?"

"Part of me would love to see Williemaye drag all these characters through hell and purgatory in court. But I think they know that," Greg speculated.

"Then what are they going to do with her?"

"Even without a plea, the church, the bank, the courts, the county would like all this to be history. I think the powers that be in Okaloosa County and the State of Florida will do as little as they can," Greg guessed.

"What's going to happen to Williemaye if she doesn't plead out before the trial tomorrow?" I asked again.

"I don't think it'll make much difference. Making an example out of her would bite too many people in sensitive places below the waist. I might be wrong but I really don't think it's going to make a difference," Greg repeated.

"What time do you want me there tomorrow?"

"The trial starts at nine, and it's going to be a circus. Be there by eight. Earlier if you want to avoid the hordes," suggested Greg.

Twenty-Five

I pulled into the overgrown driveway at Williemaye's under a full moon. I sat in the car and looked at the place where I had grown up. I couldn't bring myself to think of it as my home. It hadn't been a home when I lived there as a kid, and tonight it was just a place to sleep before testifying against my mother in court the next day. I wanted this to be the last night I ever spent in that house. Once inside, I called Heather.

"I wish I could be there with you," Heather said with conviction.

"As soon as this is over, I am out of here on the red-eye. I'll be with you before you wake up," I promised.

"I won't be sleeping when you land, I'll be at the airport. But is Greg sure that this will be over tomorrow?" she asked.

"My part will be over."

"I will say some prayers tonight and tomorrow," Heather promised firmly.

"I don't think prayer counts for much when your mother robs a church," I answered.

"Oramaye Spence would disagree with you," Heather observed.

"Between you and Oramaye, I may get lucky."

We said we loved each other, but neither one of us wanted to stop talking. She shared information about her new account and I told her about Eulah Raye. We talked for another twenty minutes before we said goodbye. I fell asleep with the cell in my hand.

I woke up late, shaved, dressed in a blur, and drove to the courthouse while trying to wake up. A half mile before I reached the courthouse, every parking spot on both sides of the street was filled. I pulled over and parked in a vacant lot that was filling up fast. I had only minutes before court started, so I walked like a man on fire to reach the court house steps. Cameras and reporters formed a phalanx around Pastor Williams. His voice carried in the steamy morning air.

"I do believe in forgiveness but I also believe in judgment. As the senior pastor at Grace Chapel, I cannot tolerate an armed robbery of my church. We are trusting Judge Hightower to administer both mercy and judgment," he thundered to the forest of cameras.

The focus on him made a way for me. Dwayne stood at the bottom of the steps telling a driver he'd best move his car before Dwayne had it towed. The driver flashed a press badge from Miami. Dwayne waved at a tow truck at the corner, and before the Miami reporter could sputter, the reporter and his car were hitched up and headed for the impound yard. Dwayne led me up the steps past a handful of reporters too busy catching the pastor's speech to notice me. I walked into the courtroom and sat next to Greg in a row right behind Mom and her attorney. They were arguing.

"Mrs. Oglesby, you've got to promise me, no outbursts," said Kaneisha in a low voice.

"Do I look like I'm gonna burst?" asked Mom loudly.

"Williemaye, you know exactly what I mean, I don't want any cussing," said Kaneisha.

"Cussing is one of the best ways I know of to deal with a situation," Mom argued.

"This is not one of those situations," replied Kaneisha.

"Well if a friggin' court ain't a fit place for cussin', I don't know where the hell is," said Mom loud enough to be heard by everyone. Nervous laughter tittered across the courtroom.

"Williemaye—Mrs. Oglesby—I hope you listen real good. If you keep this up, it will make things worse. If you can behave yourself, this may turn out much better," Kaneisha told her.

"Much better, my ass," sputtered Mom.

Kaneisha leaned close to Mom and spoke with gritted teeth. "You should plead guilty and walk out of here. I do not like our chances," she threatened.

"Hellfire and shit cakes, honey child. This is a party I'm not about to miss. I got a pile of free drinks out of this so far, and I am not going to miss the rest of this just to satisfy other people. Hell no!" said Williemaye with a grin.

I looked at the back of the courtroom. Every camera was pointed at Mom and Kaneisha, and I knew that microphones picked up every word. Clancy was fuming at the prosecutor's desk and glaring at Mom who glared back at him. It was like watching two bullies in high school staring each other down. Clancy looked away first.

Judge Hightower entered and everyone rose. Even Mom. He glanced at Kaneisha, who shook her head. His expression didn't change.

"The matter of the State of Florida versus Williemaye Oglesby is our purpose here today. Both sides have agreed that I will decide this matter without a jury in the interest of efficiency and to avoid a change of venue. I appreciate the interest of the press and public in this case, which is why I have permitted cameras in the courtroom. I would like to hear opening arguments," Hightower invited. "Would the defense make their opening statement?"

Kaneisha left the defense table to speak from the well of the court. Her brief speech was aimed not only at the judge, but the cameras as well.

"My client, Williemaye Oglesby, is an elderly resident of our community. She has chosen not to plead guilty because she believes the entire community should hear and evaluate for themselves her explanation of the events on Mother's Day. Against my advice, she insists on testifying. As her attorney of record, I must respect my client's wishes even when I disagree. I want to thank the court for the opportunity to represent an unusual client who is determined to present her side of this case."

Hightower scribbled notes while Kaneisha talked.

"That may be the shortest opening remarks I have ever heard from a defense attorney in my career," said Hightower with a smile.

Clancy stood at his table and read from a prepared text.

"Williemaye Oglesby attended Grace Chapel, the largest and most successful church in our community with one purpose, to rob the offering, the million-dollar Mother's Day offering at gunpoint. She insisted on sitting in the corner of a pew in the back of the church. A few minutes after the ushers had passed the offering plates, Williemaye found the ushers in the counting room and stuck a gun in their faces. She forced two ushers to fill a shopping bag with cash, and she had the ushers duct tape themselves to chairs in the counting room.

She finished the job and taped their mouths shut, threatening to shoot anyone who tried to break loose and follow her. She also made her son complicit in this robbery without his knowledge. Her only son came to visit her on Mother's Day, and she asked him to pick her up from church, which led to his arrest for a crime solely concocted and perpetrated by this depraved woman. No argument this woman can make can exonerate her behavior, her use of a gun, her robbery of Grace Chapel, and the media circus she has created. We are going to show the court a videotape of her televised interview at the bar where she took the press after the first hearing. The video will demonstrate that Williemaye Oglesby is guilty beyond any reasonable doubt. Her own words will serve as the best witness for the prosecution. We hope the court will agree and sentence her appropriately."

Judge Hightower looked at Clancy. "Mr. Prosecutor, call your first witness."

"The prosecution calls Lucius P. Ewell to testify," said Clancy.

I'd never seen this guy but after he was sworn in, Clancy asked him what church he attended.

"I've belonged to Grace Chapel for thirty-one years," Lucius answered.

"What do you normally do in church on Sunday mornings?" asked Clancy.

"I'm an usher."

He went on to explain that he had ushered for twenty years and knew the thousands of members on sight, and when Clancy pointed to Williemaye at the defense table and asked him had he ever seen her before, he gave a simple answer.

"First time I saw her was on Mother's Day, this year," said Lucius.

"How many people attended service on Mother's Day this year?" asked Clancy.

"We counted about four thousand people in attendance that morning."

"Out of all those people, how can you remember Williemaye Oglesby?" asked the prosecutor.

"I'm the one who tried to seat her," Lucius explained.

"You probably seated a lot of people that day. Why do you remember Williemaye?"

"I offered her a seat down front and she refused. I offered her a seat in the middle and she refused. She insisted on sitting in the back pew."

"Is that why you remember her?" asked the prosecutor.

"Before I left her in the pew, I noticed that the pew rack in front of her was short a hymnal. I asked her if she would mind if I got her one so she could sing along with everyone else."

"What did she say when you asked her about the hymnal?" asked Clancy.

"She said she'd rather puke than sing, and she told me to mind my own business."

"Did you talk to her any further?"

"I made the mistake of asking her why she wasn't wearing a corsage from the table in the foyer," said the usher.

"How did she respond to that?" asked the prosecutor with a wide smile.

"She said she'd rather I stuck the flower up my privates," Lucius responded with a red face.

"What did you do next?"

"I thought about asking her to leave but we got so busy it slipped my mind."

"When did you remember seeing Williemaye Oglesby next?" asked Clancy.

"I was in the counting room where we sort out the checks from the cash. I saw Mrs. Oglesby come through the door with a gun in her hand, and she pointed it at me."

Clancy had Lucius describe how Mom had forced him and the other three men in the room to fill her shopping bag with wads of cash from the offering plates.

"What did Mrs. Oglesby do once you had filled her bag with money?" asked Clancy.

"She pulled a roll of duct tape out of her bag and made me duct tape the other two ushers to some chairs, and then I had to mostly duct tape myself into a chair and then she finished the job."

"Did you try to talk to her while all this was happening?"

"I begged her not to do this thing. Not to rob us on Mother's Day. Told her this was a bad thing to do, to steal money from God and that God would hold her accountable," Lucius described.

"What did she say to that?"

"Said that since it was God's money, He wouldn't mind her borrowing it," answered Lucius.

"What happened next?"

"She put duct tape over everyone's mouth and left."

Clancy thanked Lucius for his testimony, and when Lucius tried to leave the witness stand, Hightower told him to sit down and wait for the cross-examination by the defense attorney.

"Why are we bothering with any more questions? That woman's as guilty as hell in a milk carton," Lucius scorned.

"Mr. Ewell, I get to decide this case. Not you, not the prosecutor, not anyone else you're ever likely to know. And you will sit in that witness chair until I tell you that you can leave. Do you understand me, Mr. Ewell?" growled Hightower.

Lucius seemed to shrink on the spot.

Kaneisha Tompkins stood at the defense table and began a crisply delivered series of questions.

"Mr. Ewell, how much money do you allege was taken on Mother's Day from the offering?"

"Ma'am, I don't quite know what you're asking," Lucius puzzled.

"I'm asking how much money was missing from the offering after this incident?" Kaneisha responded.

"I can't rightly say how much because we hadn't put it through the countin' machines yet," said Lucius nervously.

"Let's go another way then. How much were you expecting to receive that morning in the offering?" asked Kaneisha.

"We were expecting to receive at least a million dollars," answered Lucius.

"OK, then what was left for you to count after this incident?" asked the defense attorney.

"Your Honor, I don't see the point in this line of questioning. I object on the grounds that it is immaterial," Clancy protested.

"Your response, Ms. Tompkins?" asked Hightower.

"Williemaye Oglesby is accused of felony armed robbery. I would like to establish the amount she is accused of taking. I think it is exceptionally material to her defense," Kaneisha maintained.

"Overruled," boomed Hightower.

"Mr. Ewell, how much money did you count that morning after all this was over?" asked Kaneisha.

"We added up $879,456.39," Lucius sighed.

"Was most of this offering in cash?"

"Yes, it was mostly cash," answered Lucius.

"Why did people give so much cash instead of checks?" asked the defense attorney.

"We love to show the congregation what a million dollars in cash looks like at the end of the service on Mother's Day," Lucius responded.

"Has Grace Chapel ever been robbed before?" asked Kaneisha.

"Objection!" shouted the prosecutor.

Judge Hightower looked over his horn-rimmed glasses at Clancy and then at Kaneisha.

"I realize that the defendant's attorney probably wants to turn over as many stones as possible to defend her client. That's what a good attorney does, and Ms. Tompkins you are a good attorney, but this isn't going to take us anywhere that helps your client, so I am going to sustain the objection."

"Then I have no more questions for this witness," sighed Kaneisha.

"Call your next witness, Mr. Prosecutor," Hightower ordered.

"The prosecution calls Phil Oglesby," barked Clancy.

176

I had thought I'd be the last witness to testify against Mom. Hearing my name felt like a gun shot in the stomach. I was sick. I didn't move.

"Phil Oglesby, please come forward to be sworn in," Hightower instructed in his booming baritone.

Greg gave me an elbow in the ribs. I stumbled out of my seat and walked in a cold sweat to the witness stand.

"Do you solemnly swear to tell the truth and nothing but the truth, so help you God?" asked the bailiff.

"I do," I stammered.

"For the record, what is your relationship to the defendant?" asked Clancy.

"She's my mother," I answered while looking at Mom.

"Do you have any brothers or sisters?" asked the prosecutor.

"No, there's only me."

"Where's your residence?" asked Clancy.

"I live in Boston with my wife," I answered.

"Why were you here on Mother's Day?"

"I came to visit Mom."

"Was she expecting you?" asked the prosecutor.

"No, she wasn't expecting me. It was a surprise." My guts knotted up.

"How did you travel from Boston?" asked Clancy.

"I flew into Valparaiso," I answered softly.

"When did your mother know that you were in town?"

"I called her from the airport," I replied. At that question, it occurred to me that Clancy was off the script he had given Greg. Maybe it meant nothing but I didn't like it, and it made me feel even worse sitting in the witness stand looking at my mother and testifying against her for a man I detested, a man who had tried to burn my life to the ground. I hated him.

"What did she say to you when you called?" asked the prosecutor.

"She asked me to pick her up from church," I replied.

"Did you know that she went to church?" asked Clancy.

"No, I didn't know that she went to church."

"Did you know why she wanted to go to church that morning?" asked Clancy with a smirk.

"I didn't know anything about why she wanted to go anywhere that day," I answered testily.

"What church did she want you to pick her up at?" asked Clancy.

"Grace Chapel."

"Did you pick up your mother, Williemaye Oglesby, on Mother's Day at Grace Chapel?"

"Yes, I picked Mom up from Grace Chapel on Mother's Day." I looked at Mom. Our eyes met for the first time in the courtroom. She looked back at me with an odd expression that was neither love nor hate.

"Was your mother carrying anything when you picked her up?"

I heard the question but didn't answer.

"Mr. Oglesby, was Williemaye Oglesby carrying anything when you picked her up on Mother's Day at Grace Chapel?" asked the prosecutor with almost a shout.

I didn't answer.

"Your Honor, would you direct the witness to answer my question?"

"Mr. Oglesby, answer the man's question," said Judge Hightower softly.

I looked at the judge, glanced at Clancy, then stared back at Mom. I spoke to her and no one else.

"Mom, I forgive you."

"That is not an answer to my question," bellowed Clancy like someone had stuck a hot needle into one of his testicles.

"Mom, I forgive you," I repeated.

"Your Honor, may I approach the witness?" asked Clancy.

"You may," Hightower agreed.

Clancy was inches from my face and spat out his words. "You're a witness for the prosecution. Not your mother. For the prosecution! If you don't wake up and answer my questions, I am going to reinstate the charges against you and convict your ass!" he yelled. His words sucked the air out of the room until Mom boomed from the defense table.

"That prosecutor feller needs someone to take a board upside his head and beat the living shit out of him." Chuckles filled the courtroom.

Judge Hightower slammed his gavel.

"Mr. Prosecutor, you have overstepped your bounds. I don't think you need to talk to this witness anymore. You've established that the defendant asked her son to pick her up from church and that is about as far as we need to go at this time. Mrs. Oglesby, if you do that again, you will be watching this case from another room on a remote monitor with a gag in your mouth. Now, I want everyone else to simmer way down. Mr. Oglesby, this court is aware that it is not, nor should it be easy to be a prosecution witness against one's mother. That said, I want to ask you a direct question myself. Did you know that your mother was going to rob Grace Chapel that Sunday?"

I looked at Mom, who was still staring daggers at Clancy even though he was avoiding her gaze. Greg smiled at me, and I almost relaxed. "No, Your Honor, I didn't know she was going to rob anyone," I answered.

"That satisfies me. I don't think we will need to hear any more from you. Do you agree, Mr. Prosecutor?" asked the judge.

The muscles in Clancy's jaws were so tight that a quarter could have ricocheted off his face and buried itself in a wall. "I agree, Your Honor," he said between clinched teeth.

"Ms. Defense Attorney, do you have any questions for Mr. Oglesby?" asked the judge.

Kaneisha looked at me quizzically. "No."

"I like that answer. We will resume after lunch at 1:30," said Hightower.

Twenty-Six

Judge Hightower stood and everyone rose, including me, still numb from my time in the witness stand. Reporters held court in the back of the room. Clancy ignored all of them, as did Kaneisha. They took Mom out through a side door. Greg whispered into my ear before we reached the gauntlet.

"I can't say I agree with what you did, but my lawyer's gut tells me two things, Hightower likes you and you are going to be alright," he squeezed my shoulder as we reached the first rank of camera crews at the back of the court.

I stopped short of the outstretched microphones and babble of questions. Greg gave me some whispered advice, "Tell them you are glad your testimony is over, keep it short and sweet." I took a step forward.

"Did you plan to tell your mother that you forgave her from the witness stand?" asked the reporter from Court TV.

"No, I didn't plan that," I answered.

A hailstorm of questions followed my answer. Greg led me out of the courtroom, down the hallway and through the crowd on the courthouse steps, reporters and cameras at our heels and in our faces. Lucius Spence tried to make a quiet exit behind us but reporters spotted him and fell on him like an avalanche. We quickened our pace and made it to my car with no one in pursuit. We drove to Slim's Barbecue, where we ordered two pulled pork sandwiches, two sides of barbecued beans, and two quart-sized cups of sweetened iced tea at the drive through window. I drove to a vacant lot, parked beneath an old magnolia in full bloom, and ate with the windows down. The perfumed air from the trees filled the car with a sweet aroma.

"You rewrote the book on testifying against a parent this morning," said Greg between bites of his sandwich.

"I thought you were going to tell me I committed legal suicide."

"A man forgives his mother in court on national TV. Forgives a woman whose actions led to his arrest and imprisonment. Hightower was looking straight at you without a wisp of anger while you forgave Williemaye. That's a moment I will remember the rest of my life," sighed Greg.

"I hope I don't regret it the rest of mine," I answered. I looked at my watch. "We need to go back."

"Phil, Hightower as good as told Clancy to leave you alone. Kaneisha didn't call you. And isn't going to call you. You can sit this one out, if you'd like," Greg told me.

"I need to stay to the end of this."

"I think I understand. I'm mighty glad to be your lawyer for this party."

"And I'm glad to have you," I answered as I started the car.

"You don't completely understand what I'm saying," Greg suggested.

"I think you're saying you want to see how this ends," I guessed.

"Not so much that as this, Williemaye on the witness stand and Clancy asking her questions is going to be interesting. This afternoon could be one of the best afternoons any lawyer will ever see in a West Florida courtroom."

Reporters greeted me as I walked up the courthouse steps. I ignored them but things did not improve inside. Too many deputies had gone to lunch at the same time, leaving the twelve-foot-wide corridor outside the courtroom unguarded and turning it into a human sardine can; a tadpole could not have found the room to turn around.

Deputy Dwayne rescued us. He led us out the front door, through the crowd surging toward the courthouse and into the secure parking lot to the guarded side entrance. We entered the courtroom through the bailiff's door. More camera crews jostled each other for the limited space at the back of the courtroom, and a few brazen reporters tried to claim spots near the prosecution and defense tables. The bailiff, a paunchy man with a sweat-stained shirt, told the camera crews down front they would have to move to the back.

"There isn't any room in back," snarled one reporter. The bailiff waved Dwayne over. The reporters tried to argue with Dwayne, who put up with them for about two seconds.

"Y'all can leave the courtroom with your equipment or I can impound it and arrest all of you for impeding a trial. Judge Hightower likes a tidy courtroom and with y'all down here, it ain't tidy. So get your asses out of here before I have to use my pepper spray," Dwayne drawled. The crews left out the side door we had entered through.

Mom and her lawyer walked behind Clancy and his assistant. Before Mom turned to sit down, she looked Clancy in the eye and gave him a shot.

"Did you know that someone wrote a song about you?" Clancy tried to ignore her. "It mentions something about you being born an asshole," Mom chortled.

Clancy turned beet red. He dashed something on a legal pad and shoved it at his assistant, who scrambled over to the bailiff, who had his hands full trying to manage the crowd in back. The bailiff read the note and shrugged his shoulders at Clancy. Mom had won the first skirmish.

Greg leaned over and whispered to me, "If a tree falls in a forest and a judge isn't there to rule on it, did it happen?"

I understood his point. Without Hightower in the court and with the tumultuous confusion in the back, Mom knew she could insult Clancy without consequence. Hightower entered and the bailiff scurried to the front and announced, "All rise."

Hightower looked over the crowd in the back and announced, "I'm having deputies clear the hallway outside, so if anyone needs to leave for any reason, now is a good time. I expect an orderly court today." He sat down and glanced at Clancy. "Please call your next witness."

Clancy called the clerk from the Mossy Head General Store. Emma Jo seemed timid at first, answering a notch above a whisper. Hightower coaxed her into being louder. She described Mom putting cash from her shopping bag into the ATM and Mom throwing checks in the trash, checks that Emma Jo plucked out and read. The checks were all made out to Grace Chapel.

"When did you realize that this was the money that had been stolen from the church that morning?" asked the prosecutor.

"I saw the news flash on the TV that hangs in the corner. That's when I knew the money the woman was putting into the ATM was stolen," answered Emma Jo.

"Is the woman who had the shopping bag full of cash here in court today?" asked Clancy.

"Yes, she is."

"Would you point her out for the record?"

Emma Jo pointed at Williemaye. Mom ignored her. Clancy had no more questions but Kaneisha did.

"How much money did Mrs. Oglesby deposit into the ATM in your store?" asked Kaneisha.

"Objection, irrelevant," fired Clancy.

"What do you have to say about that point, Ms. Tompkins?" Hightower inquired.

"I would like someone to tell the court how much my client is alleged to have stolen because I think the specifics do matter," Kaneisha responded.

"I agree. Objection overruled. Please answer the question," Hightower instructed.

"I don't have anything to do with that ATM. We get a fee from the bank for having the ATM in our store. They take care of all the money. You'd have to ask the bank."

Kaneisha had no more questions and Emma Jo stepped done.

The bailiff rolled out a large flat screen in front of the empty jury box, and Clancy stood in front of it. "We're going to show the court the tape of the questions Williemaye Oglesby answered live at the Tropical Palms after she was released on bail," he announced. The screen sparked to life. Clancy showed fifteen minutes of Mom's performance in the bar. He replayed her statement, "I robbed the church," twice before Hightower told him to stop. Clancy took his seat and announced, "The state rests its case."

"Would the defense please call its first witness," Hightower requested.

"The defense calls Williemaye Oglesby," Kaneisha announced.

The room hummed as Mom waddled to the witness stand. The bailiff asked her to raise her hand and take the oath. "Do you solemnly swear to tell the truth and nothing but the truth, so help you God?"

"I sure as hell do plan to tell the truth!" said Mom in a booming voice that startled the court. Even Hightower took a deep breath.

"Mrs. Oglesby, do you realize that you do not need to testify?" the judge asked.

"My lawyer made that clear to me. Really clear," responded Mom.

"You can still step down if you'd like to," Hightower suggested.

"No thanks, I like the view up here," grinned Mom.

"Let's go ahead then," said the judge.

Kaneisha approached Mom and leaned against the rail as if she were talking to a friend across a fence. "You sure you want to continue?" she asked.

"Hell yes," Mom affirmed.

"Did you attend Grace Chapel on Mother's Day this year?" asked Kaneisha.

"I damn sure did."

"I don't have any more questions," said Kaneisha. Her statement stunned the court and left Clancy flat footed. Hightower had to ask him three times if he wanted to question Williemaye. When he finally said yes, the court was buzzing. Hightower pounded his gavel.

Clancy stood at his table. "Mrs. Oglesby, did you have a weapon with you when you went into the church?"

"What if I did?" Mom fired back.

"Did you have one or not?" asked Clancy.

"Probably did, always feel better when I carry a gun," answered Mom.

"Did you use this 'probably gun' to rob the church offering?" asked Clancy.

"I used a .38 special with wad cutters," answered Williemaye.

"You told this court you robbed the church to stop a foreclosure on your house. Of all the places you could have robbed, why did you choose a church? Why did you choose Grace Chapel?"

"I figured the money belonged to God and that He already had a house, a mighty big one, and all them people in that church had houses, and none of them was losing anything except me. I figured God wouldn't mind me taking what I needed. If He was upset about it, He could have stopped me with a heart attack, or a plague of locusts, or some pissed off angels that had nothing better to do. I took it as a sign from God that an old, crazy woman like me could walk into a church as big as that one, as crowded as that one, and walk out with enough money to stop them bastards, them piss-sucking vultures at the bank from taking my house," Mom snarled.

"So you think God was OK with you robbing Grace Chapel?" asked Clancy in mock amusement.

"I think God would be OK if I knocked your peter off of you and hung it on my bathroom wall!" Mom shot back. "Not that I think it would be much of a conversation piece, you being kind of stubby no matter what part of you anybody looks at," hooted Mom.

Hightower let the two go at each other like a referee at a pro-basketball game. He let them play for a minute, but he reached for his gavel just as Clancy blasted, "You old psychotic redneck bitch. We ought to lynch you right now! String you up to tallest pine we can find!"

Hightower slammed the gavel so hard it splintered. Mom looked as content as I had ever seen her, but Clancy appeared crazed. I sat next to Greg who was trying to control an ocean of laughter. He had tears in his eyes and put his head into his lap to avoid making a scene. Mom had admitted her guilt, goaded Clancy into exploding, made God a co-conspirator in her robbery, and pulled the bank into the brew. And I had forgiven this angry, furnace of a mother.

"Mr. Prosecutor, I believe that you and this witness are done!" boomed Hightower.

"Yes, we are," answered Clancy in a ghost-like voice.

"Ms. Defense Attorney, I'm guessing you don't have any re-direct for your defendant?" the judge asked.

"No, Your Honor," she answered.

"Mr. Bailiff, I want you to walk Mrs. Oglesby back to the defense table. I have an announcement to make."

Clancy didn't look her way as she made her way to her seat. Hightower looked over the audience and gave the cameras in the back a long stare. "I want everyone to take an hour break. I am going to render a verdict in this case today," he announced.

Twenty-Seven

Dwayne followed Williemaye and her lawyer out of the court-room, keeping reporters at a respectful distance. I sat with Greg as the tide of people surged out of the court. Clancy could not escape the shouted questions from the media at the back of the court. I almost felt sorry for him but he had inherited the wind, and in his duel with Williemaye, she had cut off his privates and metaphorically nailed them to her bathroom wall. He was naked before the cameras and they smelled blood. He stammered several lame excuses about the heat of the moment and not being serious about lynching Williemaye, but those words fell like turds into the punch bowl from which he was offering beverages.

Greg and I walked out of the courtroom unnoticed except for one person. Oramaye Spence caught my eye at the top of the courthouse steps and waved us over. She put her hand on my shoulder and smiled. "You did good today, Phil Oglesby."

I gave Oramaye a hug and asked, "You still think Grace Chapel should forgive her?"

"Buildings don't forgive people, but the people on the inside of them should," she replied.

"The world doesn't have enough people like you, Oramaye."

"It has more than you think. I suspect you oughta be leaving Crestview right soon now that this is over for you."

"I'm hoping to get out of here in a day or two," I answered.

"When you come back with your wife, you give me a call and I'll fix coconut cake for you again." She pecked me on the cheek and walked away at an elegant pace.

"We better get back inside, it's going to fill up in a hurry," Greg suggested.

"How much do I owe you for all this?"

"Heather gave me a retainer when she got to town. You don't owe me anything else. Hell, I'd have paid to see this," Greg announced.

"I still owe you," I affirmed.

Spectators jammed the court. The only place Greg and I could find was in the last row with the media at our backs. Half a dozen reporters found new ways to contort themselves to put microphones into my face.

"What do you expect the judge to do with your mother?" asked one reporter.

"I don't have any idea."

"Do you think your mother should go to prison?" asked another.

"That's not my decision," I responded.

"But you forgave her, right here in this courtroom this morning. Doesn't that mean you think she should go free?" asked the same reporter.

"It means I forgave her, and that's all I've got to say," I countered.

The court buzzed when Mom and her lawyer took their seats. Clancy slouched in his chair like a corpse at a wake. When the bailiff announced Hightower, silence cloaked the spectators with an edge of anticipation like static electricity. Hightower sat and began his statement.

"This is a most unusual case that has generated enormous interest locally, statewide, and nationally. I want to first address an issue of time. Both parties, the prosecution and the defense, expressed an interest in an expedited process, as did members of this community. While the media atmosphere is certainly entertaining, it does not necessarily add clarity to legal issues, whether civil or criminal. It usually adds raw emotion, the furthest thing from justice. Furthermore, both parties agreed to certain limitations in their presentations in the interest of efficiency and focus. And this court agreed, particularly after hearing from the affected parties in the religious and legal community, to consider mitigating issues as well as those that might well be regarded as aggravating.

"The court now wishes to address the remarks of the prosecutor made while questioning the defendant. Mr. Clancy, you crossed a line. I believe you have created political and legal problems for yourself that are going to distract you for quite a while. You have no one to blame but yourself. This court cannot countenance, tolerate, or abet such utterances from an attorney representing the State of Florida. No witness should ever be able to rile an attorney like the way Mrs. Oglesby riled you. You should have learned that as a first year student in law school."

"Now, Mrs. Oglesby, you have admitted your guilt, explained your motive, and shown not a shred of remorse. What you may not know is that I do have a psychiatric evaluation from one doctor and a fragment from another. Your lawyer and the prosecution agreed to add these documents to the record. Mrs.

Oglesby, you are an alcoholic with some kind of personality disorder that I cannot even pronounce. You robbed a church with a gun, and if I apply the law rigorously, you would never see daylight. Given your mental issues, your addiction problems, and requests for clemency by other interested parties, I am sentencing you to three-and-a-half years in the state hospital in Chattahoochee. At the end of that time, if you have improved, you will be on probation for five years. Do you understand this sentence?"

"I take it to mean you are locking my ass up in the loony bin for a while," Mom replied.

"That is a colorful way of putting it, so I think I could agree with your description minus a few words," smiled Hightower.

He adjourned the court with a tap of his gavel, and Deputy Dwayne led Mom out of the court.

I sat in the courtroom as the crowd choked the hallway outside. One clutch of reporters surrounded Clancy while another surrounded Kaneisha. Only a few bothered with me and Greg.

"Do you think your mother got a fair sentence?" asked one.

"I don't know what fair is anymore," was all I could think to say.

"Are you going to visit her at the state hospital?"

I didn't answer. I left the court with Greg, who followed my car to Mom's house for the last time. When we got to the driveway, we talked.

"I expected Clancy to get his ass chewed by the judge, but that's going to be his best memory from this day," Greg observed.

"Why do you think that?" I asked.

"He's about to have an ideological colonoscopy. By the time the talking heads are done with his ass, his hemorrhoids will be hanging down to his ankles. I almost feel sorry for the pompous asshole," Greg sympathized.

"What about Mom's sentence?"

"It's a Goldilocks verdict, shuts people up, stops a lot of questions."

We talked for a few more minutes, hugged like the brothers we had become, and I waved as Greg pulled out of the driveway. I stared at the house and thought about spending another night in it, but I couldn't do it. I wanted to see Heather so much that it hurt. I packed my bags and left the house keys in a broken flower pot under the porch. I drove to the airport and bought a ticket for a flight to Atlanta that would put me on a red-eye for Boston. I called Heather the moment I sat down at the gate to wait for my flight.

"Heather, I'm on my way home. Can you pick me up about midnight?"

"I'll be waiting for you," Heather answered.

"Mom got three-and-a-half years in Chattahoochee," I added.

"What do you think about that?"

"I think it could have been a lot worse."

"Are they going to leave you alone?"

"I think so. Oramaye invited us back for coconut cake."

"If I ever ask you to visit Williemaye again, take me to a psychiatrist," Heather proposed.

"I'd rather take you to bed," I invite.

Epilogue

The phone rang my third blissful day home with Heather.

"Thomas O'Brien here. I'd like to talk to Phil Oglesby," boomed a loud Boston accent.

"I'm Phil, "I said warily. More than a few nut cases had called me and I thought this was simply another crank, or journalist, or voyeur.

"I'm looking for a civil engineer. Full time staff. Are you interested?"

"Yes, I am," I stammered.

"Can you come by tomorrow, around eight in the morning? "

"Of course, what's your address?"

"O'Brien Engineering and Consulting. We're in that new tower downtown. My office is on the top floor. "

"How did you find me?" I asked.

"Saw you on TV, that court case with your mother. I believe you will fit in with our team. Look forward to shaking your hand."

He hired me the next day. I asked him a few weeks later why, of all the out of work civil engineers clamoring for jobs, he hired me. Thomas said he liked how I'd handled myself in court and that I didn't get rattled under pressure. And he added that he was a sucker for anyone who could forgive a mother who'd caused her only son to be arrested, said that made me an honorary Irishman. I'm still not entirely sure why that is true, but I love the job and work with good people every day. As for Mom, she's in Chattahoochee and still causing problems. Greg phoned to tell me that two therapists at the hospital had quit, one doctor had retired early, and four nurses were on stress leave. Kaniesha Tompkins was still at work with an appeal that seemed likely to earn Williemaye a release to a halfway house in Fort Walton Beach. Greg asked me if I had thought about visiting her. I told him that I needed to think about that.

About the Author

Ron Vincent grew up in the Florida Panhandle, the setting for Mother's Day. The dialect in the story reflects the cadences and rhythms of local speech, including profanity which, while it may seem extreme, is not exaggerated. Ron has graduate degrees in history from Texas A & M and the University of Notre Dame. He currently teaches high school in California's San Joaquin Valley.

Connect with Ron on Facebook:
https://www.facebook.com/Ronvincentauthor

Made in United States
Orlando, FL
12 May 2023

33084804R00114